Dillon glared at Mona, unable to speak.

He was overcome by a wave of nausea. The thought of her almost being shot dead turned his stomach.

"So you put your life on the line for something that probably would've still been there had you just gone back the next day with the safety of law enforcement by your side?"

Mona focused on her fidgeting hands rather than his furious stare.

"While I was out there debating what I should do next," she continued, "the attacker shot at me again. That time, the bullet almost grazed my ear."

Dillon gripped the arms of his chair and leaned forward.

"And yet, after almost being killed for a second time, you still stuck around for a necklace?"

"A necklace that may very well help solve this case."

"At the rate you're going, you won't be alive to help solve this case."

BAYOU CHRISTMAS DISAPPEARANCE

DENISE N. WHEATLEY

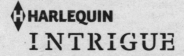

HARLEQUIN
INTRIGUE

This book is dedicated to all my fellow true crime junkies,
armchair detectives and faux forensic scientists.
Keep sleuthing, friends!

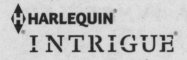

Recycling programs
for this product may
not exist in your area.

ISBN-13: 978-1-335-48930-2

Bayou Christmas Disappearance

Copyright © 2021 by Denise N. Wheatley

This edition published by arrangement with Harlequin Books S.A.

For questions and comments about the quality of this book,
please contact us at CustomerService@Harlequin.com.

Harlequin Enterprises ULC
22 Adelaide St. West, 40th Floor
Toronto, Ontario M5H 4E3, Canada
www.Harlequin.com

Printed in U.S.A.

Denise N. Wheatley loves happy endings and the art of storytelling. Her novels run the romance gamut, and she strives to pen entertaining books that embody matters of the heart. She's an RWA member and holds a BA in English from the University of Illinois. When Denise isn't writing, she enjoys watching true crime TV and chatting with readers. Follow her on social media.

Instagram: @Denise_Wheatley_Writer
Twitter: @DeniseWheatley
BookBub: @DeniseNWheatley
Goodreads: Denise N. Wheatley

Books by Denise N. Wheatley

Harlequin Intrigue

Cold Case True Crime
Bayou Christmas Disappearance

Visit the Author Profile page at Harlequin.com.

CAST OF CHARACTERS

Mona Avery—A popular investigative journalist who's covering the case of her missing former college roommate.

Dillon Reed—A devoted police detective who's the lead investigator in the missing person case.

Olivia Whitman—Mona's former college roommate, who's gone missing.

Blake Carter—Olivia's narcissistic husband, whom the public suspects is behind her disappearance. His prestigious family owns Transformation Cosmetics.

Oliver Whitman—Olivia's eccentric estranged twin brother, better known as the black sheep of the family.

Richard Boyer—Chief of police for Lake Landry, Louisiana.

Leo Mendez—Transformation Cosmetics' reputable director of operations and Blake's right-hand man.

Bonnie Young—Olivia's coworker at LLL Water Quality Laboratory.

George Williamson—An executive at Alnico Aluminum Corporation.

Chapter One

Mona Avery tightened the grip on her handbag as she hurried down the dark, hazy street.

"*Where* is that bed-and-breakfast?" she muttered into the night air.

The investigative journalist peered through the dense gray fog that had descended upon Lake Landry, Louisiana. A haunting stillness lurked along the desolate road.

She picked up speed, walking at a brisk pace. The heels on her tan suede ankle boots clicked loudly against the uneven gray pavement, reverberating through her eardrums.

A feeling of dread rumbled through her body. Mona struggled to fight it off, willing her legs to move faster as they grew heavy with angst.

She studied the shadows looming over unkempt lawns surrounding the few shuttered businesses lining the block. Not a stream of light shone from the shabby wooden structures.

Mona had arrived in Lake Landry less than a week ago to investigate the disappearance of her old college roommate, Olivia Whitman. She hadn't been back to the small, swampy town since they'd graduated.

A feeling of guilt pulled inside her chest. Mona regretted canceling their annual girls trip to Sedona, Arizona, that summer. It was a tradition they'd established years ago in an effort to stay connected.

But Mona's hectic life in Los Angeles, where she worked for the esteemed Cable News Broadcast outlet, didn't leave much time for a personal life. Keeping up with friends was a challenge. And now, it was too late. Olivia was gone.

Think positive, she told herself. *Olivia is not gone for good...*

Returning to Lake Landry should've evoked feelings of warmth and nostalgia. Mona had nothing but good memories of the town where she'd spent four years at the prestigious Emmanuel University, party hopping with Olivia while still managing to ace her courses.

But instead, she was overcome by a chilling sense of fear after her friend had disappeared.

A gust of whistling wind blew through Mona's shoulder-length curls. She brushed them away from her face, struggling to focus on the barren path ahead.

Mona had just filmed a live on-air broadcast near Olivia's last known location. When shooting wrapped, she felt anxious and hoped that the drive back to The Bayou Inn would help ease her frazzled nerves. But after the rental car ran out of gas and she decided to walk, she got turned around in the bleak, unfamiliar area.

Mona emitted a trembling groan. She loosened the belt on her chocolate brown blazer, then pressed her hand against her slender stomach, willing the nervous churn to cease.

Mona forged ahead, running the facts of Olivia's case through her mind.

Maybe that'll alleviate this eerie sense of panic...

Olivia was last seen exiting the LLL Water Quality Laboratory, where she worked as an environmental scientist. Her coworkers said she was heading to the Beechtree neighborhood to gather samples of residential water sources. When Mona asked why, she discovered that Olivia was checking for traces of lead and chromium.

Mona questioned several people who lived and worked in the dismal Beechtree area off camera. They claimed to have never seen her.

Mona decided to film her latest segment in the vicinity of the water source, hoping that the broadcast would jar someone's memory. Shortly after it ended, she received a strange text message.

Stop your investigation into Olivia Whitman's disappearance and get out of Lake Landry!

The message was disturbing to say the least. And now, as Mona hurried through the dim haze, she couldn't help but feel as though she was in danger.

Stay calm. Breathe. You're fine...

The meditative affirmations didn't help. Because Mona felt far from fine.

She curled her hands into tight fists, wondering who would have done something to Olivia. And why.

Mona as well as everyone else in town had their suspicions.

Blake Carter.

Blake was Olivia's cold, narcissistic husband. His arrogance stemmed from the wealth his family had garnered through their mega successful Transformation

Cosmetics company. He and Olivia had been together since college. Even then, Mona despised his cocky demeanor.

She'd tried to convince Olivia that she deserved better. It wasn't as if her own family didn't have their fair share of wealth. The Whitmans had collected a vast fortune thanks to Elevate Realty Group, their powerful real estate development firm.

Through the years, Blake's behavior had only worsened. Once he became president of Transformation Cosmetics, his level of egotism reached an all-time high.

But Olivia believed in the relationship and thought she could change him. So she stayed in it.

That fateful decision may have cost Olivia her life.

Mona snapped out of her thoughts as she approached the end of the pitch-black road.

She stopped abruptly.

"Oh!" Mona breathed, suddenly remembering the walking directions app on her cell phone.

She snatched the phone from her pocket and pounded the home button. The screen was blank. Her cell was dead.

"Dammit!" she screeched.

Mona resisted the urge to throw the phone down onto the ground and stomp her heel through the screen.

"Come on, come on. Where is this place…?"

She spun around, her eyes darting back and forth. Despite the steamy temperature, a piercing chill shot up her spine.

She crossed her arms in front of her and glanced up, noticing that the bulb inside of a rusted green streetlamp had burned out.

Of course, she thought while struggling to peer through the darkness.

Her head swiveled right, then left.

Which way...which way...?

Mona closed her eyes. Took a deep breath.

She opened them, made a swift left turn and hoped for the best.

Just when she thought she'd caught a glimpse of The Bayou Inn's dimly lit cedarwood sign, a pair of glaring yellow headlights sped around the corner.

A dark blue SUV careened toward her. Its lights flickered in her direction.

Mona froze.

Stinging pricks of fear shot up her calves.

The driver of the vehicle blew the shrill horn.

She recoiled and stumbled backward. Her boot's slim heel slid inside a crack in the sidewalk, causing her to fall into a lamppost.

The truck pulled toward the side of the road. Mona's eyes squinted. She struggled to see inside. But the tinted windows kept the driver's identity hidden.

When the SUV stopped right next to her, Mona reached around and gripped the lamppost.

Rusted-out edges of chipped paint scraped against her fingertips. She ignored the pain, digging deeper for fear of what was to come.

The driver slowly opened the door.

Mona held her breath, contemplating making a run for it. But her legs, leaden with fear, wouldn't allow her to budge.

She flinched at the sound of the car door slamming shut. Heavy footsteps pounded the asphalt.

"Hey, are you okay?" a deep male voice boomed.

"What do you want?" Mona screeched, cringing at the sound of alarm in her voice.

"I, uh… I noticed you out here wandering around and just wanted to make sure you're all right. Seems like you need some help."

"I—I'm fine," she stammered.

"You sure? Because you don't appear to be fine…"

The sound of footsteps drew closer. Mona backed farther into the lamppost.

"Despite what you may think," the man continued, "I'm willing to help you."

Mona held her breath. Then, she realized that the man's voice sounded familiar.

Standing in front of her was Detective Dillon Reed.

"Detective Reed!" she shrieked, pressing her hand against her forehead. "You just scared me half to death! What are you doing out here, creeping up on me like that?"

The ruggedly handsome detective's wide-set eyes lowered curiously. He chuckled, then tilted his head to the side.

"Well, first of all, my apologies," he replied smugly. "I certainly didn't mean to scare you. And I wasn't creeping up on you. Like I said, I was just checking to make sure you're okay. Now if I may ask, what are *you* doing out here? I'm surprised to see you roaming around this desolate area by yourself."

Mona dabbed the perspiration from her face and straightened her blazer. She looked directly at the detective, noticing that his full, sexy lips had curled into an amused smirk.

"You're really getting a kick out of this, aren't you?" she asked. "Are you some sort of sadist? Do you enjoy the fact that you almost gave me a heart attack just now?"

"Not at all," Dillon snorted, covering his mouth while clearly stifling a snicker.

Mona glared at him. The pair hadn't exactly hit it off since she'd arrived in Lake Landry. He was heading up Olivia's missing person investigation and feared her coverage would turn it into a media circus.

Even though he clearly didn't want her there, she couldn't seem to fight off her inherent attraction to him.

"But you still haven't answered my question," Dillon said. "What are you doing out here?"

"I just got done filming my latest news segment over by the water source where Olivia was testing for chemicals. As you know, that area was allegedly her last known location. I'm hoping the broadcast will jar someone's memory. Then as I was heading to the inn, my car ran out of gas."

Mona paused, throwing her hand on her hip while peering at Dillon.

"Wait," she continued. "You must not have checked your texts. I sent you a message last night asking if you'd be willing to go live on air with me today to discuss the case."

Or did you just choose to ignore it? she was tempted to add.

Dillon sighed deeply, running his hand over his dark, short hair.

"Mona, you already know how I feel about blasting this investigation all over the media. I'm trying to maintain the case's integrity without tainting it with the public's opinion. It's bad enough all these salacious blogs and podcasts are putting out false information."

"But the public could very well help solve this case, Detective Reed. Someone may have seen something that the authorities missed."

"Tuh," Dillon grunted, turning away from her.

Mona watched as his scowl caused wrinkles of skepticism to invade his deep brown skin. She could sense angry waves of heat coming off his body. She knew he wanted nothing more than for her to pack up and go back to Los Angeles.

Lucky for her, Dillon's boss felt differently.

Mona had forged a close relationship with Chief Richard Boyer back when she was still in college, interning at Lake Landry's local news station. He was an eager police officer who'd oftentimes acted as the department's spokesperson. Whenever the pair worked together, the chief would commend Mona's talents and predict that she'd go far in her career.

After Mona arrived in Lake Landry to cover Olivia's case, Chief Boyer welcomed her with open arms. He'd encouraged Dillon to partner with her in his investigation since she was familiar with the town and had a friendship with Olivia.

He'd initially refused. But eventually, albeit reluctantly, he gave in to the chief's request.

But Dillon had yet to really let her in. And Mona found herself struggling to crack his hardened demeanor.

"Listen, Detective," Mona said softly. "Olivia is beautiful. Her family is well-known and wealthy. Her husband's family owns one of the most popular cosmetic companies in the country. The fact that she just up and vanished is baffling. Her case is going to attract attention. Unfortunately, there isn't much you can do about that."

"Yeah, well, I can certainly try to regulate the media that comes to town trying to get me involved in their unsolicited investigations."

Mona took a step back. She opened her mouth to speak, but no words came out. She was getting tired of trying to convince Dillon that she was there to help rather than hinder Olivia's case.

"Do you know how many anonymous tips I've gotten," he began, "accusing Olivia's husband of murdering her? None of them have held any merit. Yet thanks to all the salacious media coverage, Blake Carter's name is being dragged through every mud puddle across the country. I've even had to send a squad car out to his house just to keep an eye on things."

Mona stared at Dillon and sighed.

"Well, have you bothered to look into any of those tips?" she asked. "Maybe there's some merit to them. I've got a slew of stories I could share with you about Olivia and Blake's relationship. But that would require you to actually sit down and talk with me about the case. Which you've refused to do. *Despite the chief's request for you to do so...*" she added under her breath.

"I heard that. And going off of rumors and hearsay isn't going to solve this investigation. I need solid evidence."

Mona paused, struggling to come up with a snappy comeback. But she couldn't. Because Dillon was right. She didn't have any solid evidence. *Yet.*

"Look," she told him, "all I'm saying is that two heads are better than one. I know Lake Landry. I know

Olivia. And I know Blake. Let me help you with this. I know I can—"

"May I offer you a ride somewhere, Ms. Avery?" Dillon interrupted.

Mona threw her arms out at her sides.

"So that's it? You're just gonna shut me out? Go against Chief Boyer's request that we work together on this case to try to figure out what happened to Olivia?"

He turned around and headed toward the curb.

"If you want that ride, I'll meet you in the truck."

"You have got to be kidding me," Mona muttered, watching as Dillon hopped inside the SUV and slammed the door shut.

She entertained the idea of storming off and taking her chances on getting back to the inn alone.

Don't be ridiculous, she thought. Despite being frustrated with the ornery detective, wandering around in the dark would be worse than being in his presence.

Mona strutted over to the passenger side of the truck and climbed in. She barely clicked her seat belt before Dillon peeled away from the curb and sped down the street.

"Whoa," Mona uttered, grabbing the door handle. She glanced over at him and rolled her eyes. "Sorry that my being here pisses you off so badly."

"Oh, you're far from sorry. I think you're actually happy to be here interfering in my investigation. You know, with all the cases you've covered this year, I would think you'd be eager to take a break from work and head home to Evergreen, Colorado, to spend the holidays with your family."

Mona snickered while staring straight ahead. "For

you to be so irritated by my presence, you certainly know a lot about me."

When he fell silent, she knew she'd hit a nerve. Because one thing she'd learned about Dillon, he was never at a loss for words.

"You're staying at The Bayou Inn, right?" he asked.

"Right. And way to change the subject."

"What do you want me to say?" Dillon shot back. "That I looked you up when Chief Boyer told me that some famous investigative journalist was coming to town to insert herself in my investigation? Of course I did. I guess that's just the detective in me."

Mona leaned her head against the back of her seat in exasperation.

"Come on, Dillon! I'm on your side. I wanna find out what happened to Olivia just as badly as you do. As soon as I heard that she'd gone missing, I *ran* to my boss's office and insisted that I come to Lake Landry and cover this case. When he gave me the green light, I immediately nixed my holiday plans and flew straight here."

"Humph," Dillon grumbled. He pressed down on the accelerator, the engine roaring as he flew down the winding pitch-black roads. "I wish you would've consulted with me before you canceled those plans."

She reached up and gripped the grab handle, bracing herself when the SUV careened around a corner.

"Detective Reed, I'm going to do all that I can to find out what happened to my friend, with or without your blessing. Don't forget, your boss happily welcomed me into this investigation. So I have every right to be here. Now, I can either be your biggest ally or the sharpest thorn in your side. The choice is yours."

Dillon's lips twisted with irritation. He remained silent, slowing down while approaching the inn.

Mona looked out at The Bayou Inn's beautiful yellow Victorian exterior. Its festive holiday decor was a stark contrast from the gloomy mood inside the truck.

Lush evergreen wreaths adorned with bright gold bows lined the windows. Sweet-smelling garland made of fresh eucalyptus, bay leaves and red berries hung from the porch's white railings. Colorful icicle string lights flickered along the roof's shingles. The majestic Atlas cedar that stood in the middle of the yard twinkled with sparkling lights, highlighting the tree's silvery blue foliage.

For Mona, staying at the inn felt bittersweet. On one hand, it brought back fond memories of her college years. But on the other hand, it was a constant reminder that Olivia was gone.

The Whitman family owned The Bayou Inn. During their time at the university, the two friends earned extra cash by working there on weekends.

They'd help prepare the ornately decorated rooms for guests by setting up welcome gift baskets and dusting off the beautiful Parisian furnishings, contemporary artwork and low-country antiques.

Mona was jolted out of her thoughts when Dillon stopped in front of the entrance.

Just as he put the truck in Park, a streak of lightning flashed across the sky. It was followed by a roaring crackle of thunder, then a sudden downpour of rain.

"Oh *wow*," Mona gasped, staring out at the torrential shower as raindrops crashed against the windshield.

"Oh wow is right. Looks like I came to your rescue

just in time. Imagine roaming around out there in the dark and then, *boom*! A monsoon hits."

Mona waved off Dillon's dramatics and grabbed her purse. "I'm sure I would've survived. But nevertheless, thanks for the ride."

Before she opened the door, Dillon put the truck in Drive and tapped the accelerator, making sure that he was parked directly underneath the inn's awning.

"So you won't get wet," he told her.

Mona paused, surprised by the considerate gesture.

"Thanks," she responded quietly. "I appreciate it."

Dillon's softened expression left her wondering whether she should invite him inside. Moments alone with him like this were rare. She wanted to take advantage of it. Maybe he'd open up to her in front of the inn's cozy fireplace over a mug of hot apple cider and a plate of Cajun ginger cookies.

What do you have to lose? she asked herself. *Just go for it...*

Mona turned to him and cleared her throat. "Hey, would you like to—"

Before she could finish, Dillon's cell phone rang.

"Excuse me," he said, reaching down into the cup holder and grabbing his cell.

Mona slumped back into her seat, instinctively knowing that the chance to invite him in had passed her by.

"Detective Reed," he said into the phone. "What's up, Officer Freeman?...Yes, Olivia's car was recovered outside of Jefferson Parish...Exactly. Nowhere near the area where she went missing...We did turn it over to Forensics. Came back clean...Oh, you got a new tip? What time did it come in?...Yeah, we should definitely look into it now. I'll swing by the station and pick you up in a few. Thanks."

Dillon disconnected the call and turned to Mona. "I need to get going. But before I leave, a word of advice. Be sure to keep that gas tank full."

"Do you think that tip you just received will lead to some solid evidence?" Mona asked, ignoring his unsolicited suggestion. She crossed her fingers underneath her purse, hoping Dillon would give in and share the details.

"I don't know yet. We'll see."

She waited for him to elaborate. When he didn't, she parted her lips to ask another question. But before she could, Dillon threw open his door and hopped out of the truck.

He jogged over to the passenger side and opened her door. Mona just sat there staring at him, irritated that the conversation had ended so abruptly.

He extended his hand in an attempt to help her out of the truck. She ignored it, climbing out on her own and brushing past him.

"Oh, so it's like that?" he asked.

Mona spun around and faced him. "Yes. It's definitely like that. You set the tone, Detective. I'm just following your lead. But like I said, I'm going to be involved in this investigation whether you like it or not. I'll actually be down at the station tomorrow to meet with Chief Boyer."

"But…*why*?"

"Thanks again for the ride," Mona told him, ignoring his question. "Have a good night."

And with that, she swiveled on her heels and strutted toward the inn's white wooden door.

Right before going inside, Mona glanced back at Dillon. He was still standing there, a stern expression on his face as he watched her walk away.

Stay on the case, she told herself, now even more determined to find Olivia. *With or without Dillon's help...*

Chapter Two

Dillon sat down and slid his rolling mesh chair closer toward his cluttered cherrywood desk. Normally the messy files strewn about and printouts of his latest reports were neatly tucked away in a drawer. But ever since he'd begun investigating Olivia's disappearance, he couldn't seem to keep organized.

Dillon had arrived in Lake Landry a couple of months ago by way of Baton Rouge's police department. After ten years of working on its force, the city's high crime rate had finally gotten the best of him.

He'd made the move to Lake Landry in hopes of settling into a quieter, more peaceful life. The last thing he had expected was for a high-profile missing person case to land on his desk. But that's exactly what happened when Chief Boyer named him lead detective in the Olivia Whitman investigation.

"Are you sure about this?" Dillon remembered asking the chief. "You've got a couple of detectives in this department who grew up in Lake Landry and know Olivia's family very well, along with her husband's. Don't you think one of them would be better suited to take the lead on this case?"

"Those are all the reasons why they *wouldn't* be better suited to handle this case," the chief had rebutted. "These guys are too close to the Whitman and Carter families. They all have preconceived notions on Olivia's disappearance. Who did it. Why it was done. I need a fresh, unbiased mind on this."

"But, sir, I literally just arrived in Lake Landry. I don't know the town. I don't know the people. I'm not familiar with—"

"Your unfamiliarity with this town and everyone in it could very well be the key to solving the case," Chief Boyer interrupted. "Not to mention your impeccable track record in Baton Rouge. I don't have that level of experience here in this town. So congratulations, Detective Reed. You're it."

Dillon had just stood there in the chief's office, peering at the enthusiastic grin on his round, jovial face. As Chief Boyer stared back at him, silently running his chubby hand over the gray stubble on his cheeks, Dillon realized the decision was final.

The dinging of Dillon's email inbox snapped him out of his thoughts. He ignored the incoming message and grabbed the photos of the area where Olivia had allegedly gone missing, studying every angle closely.

The dark water appeared still, almost haunting. Barren branches hung from the shrubbery, skimming the lake's edge. When Olivia disappeared, the first thing Dillon had done was hire rescue divers to search the water. Thankfully, her body hadn't been recovered.

"Come on, Olivia," he muttered. "Talk to me. Where are you? What happened to you?"

He examined the pictures for several minutes, struggling to discover a new clue. When nothing jumped out at him, he turned to his laptop and pulled up the internet.

"CNBNews.com," he said aloud, typing in the web address to Mona's network.

CNB's blue-and-white pyramid logo appeared on the screen. Dillon hovered the cursor over the menu prompt. He searched for a list of journalists, then double-clicked on Mona's name.

"Latest broadcast," he mumbled, tapping on the video she'd shot near the Beechtree residential water source the night before.

When Mona's image popped up on the screen, Dillon felt a sizzling burn ignite in the pit of his stomach. *Come on, dude*, he told himself. *Chill out...*

Dillon still remembered the moment Chief Boyer walked Mona into his office to introduce the pair. He'd been given a heads-up that she would be arriving in Lake Landry to cover Olivia's case.

Dillon didn't hold back when telling the chief she was not welcome in his investigation. But Chief Boyer had a soft spot for Mona. He'd watched her go from an eager small-town network intern to a reputable, hot-shot LA journalist.

In the end, Dillon had no choice but to accept his boss's wishes.

What he didn't expect was the jolt of sexual energy that shot through his body when the beautiful journalist sauntered up to his desk.

He'd looked her up online prior to her arrival and was aware of her obvious beauty. But in person, Mona's cascading jet-black curls, flawless caramel-toned skin, brown doe eyes and pouty lips took the normally cool detective's breath away.

Dillon somehow managed to hide his admiration while watching her long, lean legs, which were covered in black leather leggings that day, move with the grace of a ballerina.

When Mona spoke, her voice resembled that of a charismatic radio host while she carried the look of a runway model. Both her confidence and intelligence were apparent, as was her passion for finding Olivia.

A lesser man would've easily been intimidated. But not Dillon. In that moment, his irritation overrode his awe. Rather than thinking of ways to get to know her better, he was contemplating ways to send her packing.

The sound of Mona's broadcast boomed from Dillon's speakers, bringing him back to the present. He focused on the screen.

"Take a good look at this location where I'm standing," Mona said into the camera.

Her knuckles appeared white as she gripped the microphone. The protruding vein running down the middle of her forehead revealed her concern.

"If you remember seeing anything out of the ordinary in this area the day that Olivia Whitman went missing," Mona continued, "or have any information on her disappearance, I urge you to please call local authorities. The telephone number to the anonymous tip line is running along the bottom of the screen."

As Dillon continued watching the broadcast, he felt his mouth go dry. He grabbed his mug of black coffee and went to take a sip. When nothing but air flowed through his lips, he realized the cup was empty.

"I'm Mona Avery, signing off. Until next time, remember, if you see something, say something."

Dillon stared at the screen until the video went black.

He sat there for a moment, gathering himself before heading to the break room for his third cup of coffee.

"Hey, Detective Reed!"

Dillon's shiny black oxford shoes screeched along the wooden floor when he came to an abrupt halt. He spun around and glanced inside Chief Boyer's office.

"Can I see you for a quick sec?" the chief asked.

"Of course."

Dillon strolled through the doorway, stepping carefully through the stacks of files lining the floor.

"Be careful. Don't slip on those piles. Mildred is reorganizing my cabinets. Close the door and have a seat, will you?"

Uh-oh, he thought. Whenever the chief asked him to step into his office, close the door and have a seat, he usually followed up with something Dillon didn't want to hear.

"What's going on, sir?" Dillon asked after slowly sitting down across from him.

"Well, I wanted to follow up with you on the Olivia Whitman investigation. How's it going?"

"It's going. I've been meticulously reviewing all the evidence that I've collected and pursuing new leads. Officer Freeman and I followed up on a tip we received that sounded pretty promising, too."

"Oh yeah?" Chief Boyer asked, his unruly salt-and-pepper eyebrows shooting up toward his forehead. "What did it entail?"

"There was an alleged sighting of Olivia at the King Cake Café. So Freeman and I went to the bistro, questioned some of the workers and patrons, and reviewed surveillance footage. Unfortunately, nothing came of it."

"Hmm…" Chief Boyer propped his hands underneath his chin and rested his elbows on his chair. "What about Mona? Have you two had a chance to sit down and discuss the case yet?"

Dillon's gaze diverted from the chief's probing stare and focused on his training certificates hanging along the back wall.

"I, uh—we've chatted a bit here and there, but, um…" Dillon's voice trailed off. Silence filled the office.

Chief Boyer lowered his head and eyed Dillon over the top of his black rectangle bifocals.

"Listen, Reed. Mona is a top-notch investigative journalist. Her skills are impeccable, bar none. She's helped law enforcement agencies all over the country solve some pretty complicated cases. Now, I know you're a proud detective who's capable of handling this investigation on your own. But this is a high-profile case that just so happens to be close to my heart. We need all the help we can get to solve it as quickly as possible."

"But, sir, I don't need some—"

"With all due respect, Detective," the chief interrupted, "this isn't up for debate. This is an order."

The finality in Chief Boyer's low tone convinced Dillon that the conversation was indeed over. There was no way out of this. He was officially stuck working with Mona.

Dillon slumped down in the hard wooden chair and swiped his thumb along his perspiring brow. As he waited for his boss to dismiss him, there was a knock at the door.

Chief Boyer glanced up at the clock, then over at Dillon. When the chief tightened his lips and nodded his head, Dillon automatically knew who was on the other side.

Mona Avery.

"Come in!" Chief Boyer called out.

Dillon gripped the arms of his chair. He clenched his jaws as the creaking door slowly opened.

"Good morning, gentlemen."

The sound of Mona's silky voice flowed through his eardrums. He shifted in his seat and inhaled sharply.

"Detective Reed," she continued. "This is a surprise. I didn't expect to see you in our meeting."

"Yeah, neither did I," Dillon shot back defensively, swiveling in his chair. When he laid eyes on her, his demeanor immediately softened.

Mona looked beautiful, almost angelic, dressed in a cream suede blazer and fitted cream pants. Her hair was wrapped in a bun, with soft tendrils framing her face. Matte red lipstick highlighting her perfectly straight teeth. The subtle scent of rose perfume floated through the stuffy office.

Dillon felt himself growing mesmerized by her presence.

Stop it! he told himself, irritated by his uncontrollable reaction.

"Good morning, Mona," Chief Boyer boomed. "Please, have a seat. Can Detective Reed get you anything? Coffee? Tea? Water?"

Dillon's head jerked toward the chief. He noticed a glimmer of mischief in his boss's eyes.

"No, thank you," Mona replied. "I'm fine. I think I drank a whole pot of coffee earlier this morning back at the inn."

"Oh yeah," Chief Boyer uttered, rubbing his hands

together. "Isn't The Bayou Inn's manager, Evelyn, serving up their holiday blend this time of year? Medium roast with touches of cinnamon and vanilla?"

"Yes, sir, she is," Mona responded before she and the chief chuckled in unison.

Dillon groaned underneath his breath, annoyed with their friendly banter.

"Hey," Chief Boyer continued, "I was just asking Detective Reed whether you two have had a chance to sit down and discuss Olivia's case yet. He's informed me that you in fact have not. So we're gonna work to make that happen. Isn't that right, Detective?"

Dillon turned to Mona. She stared back at him, the slight smirk on her face oozing with self-satisfaction.

"Yes, sir," he said stiffly. "That's right…"

"Good. Now, Mona, you said you've got some information on Olivia's husband, Blake, that you wanted to share with me?"

"I do."

Dillon watched as she pulled a leather binder from her tote bag and placed it on the desk.

"So as you both know," Mona began, "Blake Carter is one of the main suspects in this case."

"That has not been made official," Dillon interjected. "We have yet to name any suspects or persons of interest in this case."

"Okay," Mona replied. "Well, let me rephrase that, then. Hypothetically speaking, Blake *may* be a suspect in this case."

When Dillon opened his mouth to speak, Chief Boyer held up his hand. "Please. Let her finish."

Dillon resisted the urge to jump up and walk out of

the office. Instead he sat back in his chair and tightened his lips in frustration.

"Look," Mona continued, "all I'm saying is that I think we should take a closer look at Blake. There are so many things he's done, even before Olivia disappeared, that seem suspicious."

"And I'm assuming you have a list of those things tucked away in your little binder?" Dillon asked sarcastically.

"As a matter of fact, I do. First of all, Blake—"

Mona was interrupted by a knock at the door.

"Hold that thought," Chief Boyer told her before calling out, "Yes?"

Dillon turned around and saw Officer Freeman stick his head in the doorway.

"Sorry to interrupt. Chief, the officers are in the briefing room waiting on you."

"Waiting on me for what?" he asked before turning toward his computer and clicking on the mouse. "Oh! I forgot I've got the ethics training update."

Dillon watched as the chief grabbed his notebook and jumped up from behind the desk.

Thank goodness...he thought, grateful for the interruption.

"Mona, Detective Reed, I'm so sorry. But I've gotta cut this meeting short. I'll tell you what. Why don't you two continue this conversation over an early lunch? Then I'll circle back with the both of you later."

Dillon clenched his teeth at the thought of having to sit across from Mona, one-on-one, and discuss a case he wished to keep close to the vest.

When he glanced over at her, he sensed that she felt the exact same way as she shoved her papers back inside the binder. Her movements were stiff and expression was tight.

"No worries, Chief," Mona uttered. "Hopefully you and I can reschedule our meeting. I'd still like to go over my thoughts on Olivia's disappearance with you."

Dillon almost felt guilty underneath the weight of her strained tone.

You've gotta lighten up, man, he told himself.

But when a wave of doubt overcame him, he gripped the arms of his chair and stood up.

Or at least try...

"I look forward to hearing your thoughts on the case, Mona," Chief Boyer told her. "But in the meantime, go ahead and share them with Detective Reed. I have no doubt that if the two of you put your heads together, you'll have this case solved in no time."

And with that, the chief shuffled out the door.

"So, um," Dillon began, his voice cracking awkwardly, "are you hungry?"

"I could eat." Mona shrugged. She slipped her binder inside her tote without making eye contact with him. "Do you have a taste for anything in particular?"

As Mona stood up, Dillon rushed to pull out her chair. "I was actually thinking of getting a spicy grilled shrimp salad from The Weeping Willow Bistro."

"Mmm, that sounds good. Weeping Willow's has the best hot water corn bread and mango lemonade in town."

"I have to agree with you there."

Dillon watched as Mona sauntered out of the office. The sight of her long, lithe legs caused a tingling to swirl inside his chest.

He coughed loudly and followed her toward the exit.

"After my experience last night," she said, "I made sure to fill up the gas tank on my rental. So I can just drive over to the bistro and meet you there."

"No need for that," Dillon blurted out before thinking twice. "Just leave your car here. I can drive us, then bring you back after we're done."

Mona stared at him through wide eyes. It was obvious his suggestion had come as a surprise. Hell, the idea had even shocked him.

What are you doing? he asked himself. *You're slipping, man...*

"Are you sure?" she asked, her high-pitched tone filled with uncertainty. "I don't want to inconvenience you."

"It's no inconvenience at all. Should we head out?"

"Yep. Let's go."

MONA TOOK A bite of her corn bread and closed her eyes. "Mmm, this is good. Oh, how I've missed it. By the time I get back to LA, I'll probably be a good ten pounds heavier."

"I highly doubt that," Dillon said, discreetly eyeing her slim figure. "It's obvious you take great care of yourself."

"Thank you. I try."

An awkward silence fell over the pair. Dillon curled his hands into tight fists underneath the table, hoping his comment hadn't come across flirtatiously.

He took a sip of lemonade and glanced around the lively Cajun-style restaurant. Crowds gathered around the redbrick walls, admiring glittery feathered Mardi Gras masks. Patrons were seated in pub stools, their distressed wooden high-top tables overflowing with platters of boiled crawfish and bowls of jambalaya.

"So tell me, Detective Reed," Mona asked, "what brought you to Lake Landry? From what I've heard, you were next in line to becoming chief of police back in Baton Rouge."

Dillon felt his hands slowly unravel. He was seldom rattled by the presence of others, if ever. He chalked it up to working in law enforcement for so many years.

But there was something about Mona that knocked him off his square.

"From what you've heard?" he asked. "Does that mean you've been asking about me?"

The right corner of Mona's lips curled into a slight smile. "Maybe. Well, actually...yes."

"Oh, okay. Now see, I wasn't the only one making inquiries. You were asking about me, too, huh?"

"It wasn't even like that, Detective. I had to know who I'd be partnering with after Chief Boyer sang your praises. Or who I *thought* I'd be partnering with..."

A sliver of guilt jabbed at Dillon's side. His eyes squinted thoughtfully as he watched Mona stare down at her plate, stabbing a piece of romaine lettuce with her fork.

"To answer your question," Dillon said, "the high rate of violent crimes occurring back in Baton Rouge got to be too much for me. I needed a slower pace. I thought a smaller, quieter town would help lower my anxiety level *and* blood pressure. And I'm single, so I figured the move would be easy. But then, the minute I get to town, *boom.* I'm assigned a case that's caught the attention of the entire nation."

"Lucky for you, you've got help all around you.

Lake Landry's police department is extremely capable. They've always had an all-hands-on-deck type of attitude. At least they used to."

"And they still do. I'm getting plenty of input from other officers. And I'm open to it. But I'm the lead detective in Olivia's case. So at the end of the day, I'm going to investigate it my way."

"Understood. But I do have some information on Olivia's husband, Blake, that you may not know."

"And what would make you think that?"

Mona leaned into the table and tapped her index finger in front of Dillon.

"Blake Carter comes from a powerful family, Detective. People in this town are afraid of him. He's always been a cold narcissist who thinks his money can buy him out of any situation. They don't want to get involved and end up like Olivia."

"That's why we've got the anonymous tip line," Dillon told her. "If the townspeople feel uneasy speaking with law enforcement directly, they should feel comfortable utilizing it."

"It's not that simple. The townspeople believe that some members of law enforcement are on Blake's payroll."

"Oh, come on," he huffed, throwing up his hand. "Look, I may be new to Lake Landry PD, but I don't believe that for one second. This town's police department is known for having a pristine reputation throughout the state of Louisiana. Now, you claim to know things about Blake that I don't. What would those things be? Because I know plenty."

Mona crossed her arms in front of her. "Did you

know that Blake wasn't seen around Transformation Cosmetics' offices the day that Olivia went missing?"

Dillon paused. He'd heard all about how Blake was an egotistical maniac who arrogantly flashed his wealth and mistreated his wife. But he didn't know the man hadn't shown up for work that day.

"Are you sure?" he asked skeptically. "Because Blake stated he was at work. And Blake's executive assistant was one of the first people I questioned after I spoke to him. She assured me he was in the office all day."

"Did she really," Mona uttered sarcastically, tilting her head to the side. "So I guess you also haven't heard that Blake and his assistant Ayana are having an affair. In addition to a couple of other women within the company."

Dillon leaned back in his chair, his eyes fixated on Mona's knowing expression. *"Wow,"* he breathed. "Are you serious?"

"Very. See why teaming up with me might not be such a bad thing? I have access to inside information swirling around town that you simply don't, Detective Reed."

He just sat there, dumbfounded. His lips parted, but nothing came out. Because he realized that Mona just might be right.

Dillon propped his elbow on top of the table and fidgeted with his perfectly trimmed goatee. He studied Mona's face, searching for any signs of salaciousness or deceit. He saw none. Her look of determination appeared pure. He could sense that she was really there to help find her friend rather than gain more popularity through sensational reporting on the case.

"You, um…you may be right, Ms. Avery. Maybe I could use your assistance with this investigation. But if I do agree to this partnership, it's gonna come with some terms and conditions."

"Such as?"

"Well, first off, you have to stop referring to me as Detective Reed and start calling me Dillon."

"Deal. So long as you call me Mona instead of Ms. Avery."

"You got it. Second, I'm going to need for you to keep in mind that this is *my* investigation. I take the lead on this case. And what I say goes. While I do respect your opinion and I'm open to hearing you out, I don't want us bumping heads and debating nonstop. We have to work together. Respectfully."

"I can do that," Mona replied, tapping her rose-colored fingernails against the glass of lemonade. "What else?"

"Third, and most important, no going behind my back and conducting your own personal investigations. You need to keep me in the loop on whatever plans you have to speak with people and search certain areas."

As soon as the words were out of Dillon's mouth, Mona threw her head back and stared up at the ceiling.

"Come on, now," she moaned. "Are you serious? I'm an investigative journalist, Dillon. This is what I do."

"Not on my watch. Once again, this is *my* investigation. So we're going to do things my way. This can get dangerous, Mona. I know that all eyes are on Blake right now, but we don't know if he's truly behind Olivia's disappearance. So, until we figure out exactly who and what we're dealing with, I'm making it my responsibility to keep you safe. Understand?"

Dillon almost laughed out loud as he watched Mona squirm in her chair. Clearly she wasn't used to being told what to do.

"Fine," she blurted out. "But do I even have any other choice?"

"Nope. You don't."

Just when Dillon took the last bite of his salad, their server approached the table.

"How's it going, you two?" she asked through a toothy grin. "Are those salads and slices of corn bread making those taste buds happy?"

"Ecstatic," Mona told her, placing her hand over her stomach. "Everything was delicious. I almost ordered another slice of corn bread. But I figured I'd better stop while I'm ahead."

"Would you two like a cup of coffee? Or how about a plate of dessert? We're serving up bananas Foster, pecan pralines, king cakes…"

"Mmm, sounds amazing," Dillon said, "but I'm going to have to pass. Mona? Would you like anything?"

"I'd better not. I'll definitely be back for a bowl of bananas Foster before I leave town, though."

"Oh, we've got a tourist!" the server chirped, her Southern drawl dripping with cheer. "What brings you to town?"

Before Mona could respond, the woman gasped and pointed at her.

"Wait a minute, I knew I recognized you from somewhere! You're Mona Avery! I always watch your broadcasts. Honey, let me tell you, I am a true-crime fanatic."

"Aww, well, thank you. I appreciate that."

The server dropped her arms down by her sides and

stared directly at Dillon. "I really do hope you two nail that Blake Carter. All of Lake Landry knows he did something to that sweet wife of his."

Dillon quickly cleared his throat and held up his finger. "If you wouldn't mind bringing us the check, that would be great. Thanks."

He noticed the server's hands trembling when she reached up and tucked a strand of hair behind her ear.

"Comin' right up," she muttered, side-eyeing him before slinking off.

"Oh boy," Mona sighed. She tossed her napkin down onto the table. "We've got our hands full with this case and the townspeople. I'm telling you, the Whitman family is loved by this community. And Olivia is like a star in Lake Landry. I was in awe of her when we first met. Funny how her twin brother Oliver is the complete opposite."

"Yeah, what's up with him? I've tried to get him to come down to the station on numerous occasions. I thought he'd be happy to share some insight into Olivia's disappearance with me. But so far he's been completely uncooperative."

Mona shook her head and stared down at the table.

"That doesn't surprise me. Oliver is the black sheep of the Whitman family. Oddly enough, he seems to relish in that. He attended college with us for one semester but dropped out after that."

"He's definitely a bit strange. What was he like back when you were living here?"

"Oliver's always been this detached loner who wasn't interested in academics. He always said he'd rather attend the school of life, as if he was too good for a traditional education. But he never had any real goals or aspirations. The only thing he was interested in was laying up in his parents' mansion and playing video games."

"Well, from what I've heard, the Whitmans are fed up with Oliver. They forced him to get a job in Transformation Cosmetics' warehouse."

Mona threw her head back and laughed profusely. "The thought of Oliver doing any sort of manual labor is hilarious. I'm actually surprised he's lasted this long at the company."

"Lucky for him, his brother-in-law runs it."

"I know, right? Without that little perk, I seriously doubt he would've even gotten the job." Mona paused, peering at Dillon from across the table. "You asked for full disclosure when it comes to Olivia's case, right?"

"I did. Why?"

"Well, *full disclosure*, Blake has agreed to meet with me this afternoon. I told him I just want to have a casual conversation. As old friends."

"Okay. What time are we meeting with him?" Dillon asked.

Mona's eyes shifted around the restaurant. "*I'm* scheduled to meet with him at two o'clock."

"Didn't we just talk about this? I don't want you conducting these little side investigations on your own. It's not safe, Mona. Can't you understand that?"

"Of course I understand that. But Blake and I go way back. Now, is he a jerk? Absolutely. We haven't always been on the best of terms. I've checked him on numerous occasions over the way he's treated Olivia. But he would never—"

She paused when the server set the check down on the table.

"Thanks again for stopping in," she mumbled. Gone was the chipper tone in her voice. "Looking forward to that arrest being made…"

"Thank you for everything," Mona quickly interjected before Dillon could respond. "Detective, are you ready to go?"

"Definitely."

He pulled out his wallet and paid the bill, then followed Mona toward the exit.

Once the pair were outside, he inhaled the warm, humid air, squinting in the bright sunlight.

Christmastime in Lake Landry was in full swing. The sound of festive music lingered in the breeze. Local stores lining the streets were heavily decorated with colorful ornaments. Shoppers carrying bags filled with gifts packed the walkways.

But despite all the merriment, Dillon was completely unplugged from the holiday season. The only thing on his mind was finding Olivia.

"So where are you meeting Blake?" he asked Mona as they approached his car.

"At Kimmy's Coffee and Cake Shop. It's right across the street from Transformation Cosmetics."

"Yeah, I know that place."

Dillon wanted to revisit the idea of Mona not going alone. But he knew the suggestion would fall on deaf ears.

He opened the passenger door. Mona stepped forward, pausing before slipping inside. Her hand brushed against his when she gripped the doorframe. He swallowed the stream of heat that shot up his throat.

The pair locked eyes. Dillon noticed a fiery look

in Mona's gaze, as if she were still waiting for him to challenge her meetup with Blake.

Just back off, he told himself. *Let the woman do her thing.*

"I—" both Dillon and Mona said simultaneously.

They paused, emitting awkward chuckles.

"Please," Dillon said, "may I speak first?"

"Of course."

"Thank you. Now, if I'm being honest, I am not comfortable with you meeting Blake alone."

"But I—"

Dillon gently placed his hand on her shoulder, quieting her.

She jumped slightly, appearing surprised.

"Sorry," he blurted out, quickly removing his grasp. He cleared his throat, then continued.

"I understand that you and Blake go way back. You two have established a rapport. Honestly, you may be able to get more out of him than I did. So, with that being said, I'll give you a pass and let you meet up with him. *This* time."

"Oh gee, thanks," Mona quipped.

She climbed inside the car and grabbed the door handle. After a silent staredown, Dillon backed away.

Just leave it alone, he told himself before getting in and pulling off.

"Look, Dillon, you seem skeptical of every move I make. Now, I may not be a law enforcement officer, but I am a very capable, experienced investigative journalist. My track record speaks for itself."

"That it does. And listen, it's not that I'm skeptical. It's just… I'm not used to partnering up with anyone outside of law enforcement. Especially someone linked to the media. I had several run-ins with Baton Rouge's news outlets during some of the most important investigations of my life. I don't wanna keep going through that. It's one of the reasons why I left the department."

"I understand that. But I work for a very reputable news outlet. And have you researched the cases I've worked on? Trust me, you're in good hands."

Dillon nodded his head while turning down Statewood Avenue. He had in fact looked into Mona's previous casework. And it was impressive to say the least.

She had assisted law enforcement agencies all over the United States in solving numerous investigations, from human trafficking rings to murder-for-hire plots. Her skillset and contributions could not be denied.

"Okay," Dillon said. "I'll fall back on this meetup with Blake. Just promise me you'll reach out as soon as it's over and let me know how it went."

"I will absolutely do that. And hopefully this is just the beginning. My main goal is to get an on-air interview with him. Maybe seeing his face on national television will encourage people who know more than what they're saying to come forward."

"If only it were that easy…"

Chapter Three

The silver bell hovering over Kimmy's Coffee and Cakes' white wood-framed door jingled loudly.

Mona glanced up at the entrance, expecting to see Blake enter the café. But instead a group of chatty mothers and their young children walked inside.

The pastel-themed sweet shop was packed. Charming curved metal tables and chairs with red bows tied across their backs were filled with Christmas shoppers. Twig wreaths intertwined with holly hung from the walls. A silver tree adorned with crystal ornaments stood in the front window. And trays of mocha lattes, hot chocolate and pastries were being served to the festive patrons.

Mona checked the time. It was almost 2:30 p.m. Blake was practically thirty minutes late. She grabbed her cell phone, opened their text message thread and began typing.

Hey, I'm at Kimmy's. Been here since 2. Are you still planning on meeting—

The bell over the door jingled again. Mona's head shot up. Blake finally came strolling through the door.

In all the years she'd known him, nothing had changed. Judging from the size of his biceps, which appeared well-defined underneath his dark gray blazer, Blake had still been hitting the gym religiously. His dark hair and perfectly trimmed mustache appeared freshly cut. She raised her hand and caught his attention. He looked over and nodded his head, then made a beeline toward her table.

All eyes were on Blake as he swaggered through the café. Mona had chosen a table in the back corner, hoping they'd have some privacy. But considering the size of the small shop, discretion was practically impossible.

He appeared oblivious to the patrons' stares and whispers, staring straight ahead while he made his way through the maze of tables. But judging from the slight smirk on his face, he was aware of the attention and seemed to enjoy it.

Typical Blake...

Mona stood up when he approached her table.

"Well, well, well," Blake said, his deep voice tinged with a touch of cynicism. "If it isn't the infamous Mona Avery. How've you been, M-Boogie?" he asked, referring to her old college moniker.

"I'm hanging in there," she replied coolly. "How are you?"

"I'm doing all right, considering the circumstances."

Mona cringed slightly when he reached out and embraced her. She barely wrapped her arms around him before patting his back, then quickly stepping away.

When Blake adjusted the gold links attached to his crisp white cuffs, Mona noticed his manicured hands and his diamond-embellished luxury watch.

Just as flashy as ever, Mona thought.

He gripped a chair and pulled it away from the table, flinching at the sound of its clawed feet screeching against the white marble floor.

It was then that Mona realized Blake wasn't as composed as he appeared.

"Are you okay?" she asked.

He slowly sat down and folded his hands on top of the table. "I'm just trying to maintain some sense of normalcy in the midst of all this madness. My wife is missing. Almost everybody in town suspects that I had something to do with it. Which of course I didn't."

Mona took a seat across from Blake. She studied his expression. Gone was the arrogant smirk. It'd been replaced by a tight frown. His face was lined with worry. She was surprised by his outward show of concern. Blake had never been the type to let people see him sweat.

But it could all just be an act, she told herself.

"Well," she sighed, "I am so sorry that this has happened. We're all hurting over Olivia's disappearance. That's why I'm here. I'm going to do all that I can to help get to the bottom of this and bring Olivia home safely."

"And I appreciate that. Hopefully you'll be adding this case to your long list of success stories."

"Let's hope so," Mona replied, side-eyeing Blake skeptically. She still couldn't get a grasp on whether or not he was being sincere. "You and I certainly have a lot to catch up on."

"That we do," Blake muttered before glancing down at his watch. "But unfortunately, we may have to save some of that catching up for another day. I've got a meeting with a new PR consultant that my director of operations set up in twenty minutes."

"*Twenty minutes?* That won't give us enough time to talk."

"Sorry," he said with a shrug, sitting back in his chair. "It'll have to do for now. We're preparing for Transformation Cosmetics' annual Christmas toy drive, and this year's event is gonna be huge. It's even being covered by the national news."

There he is, Mona thought. *Back to the Blake I know. All about the business and his image.*

"I don't know if you're familiar with the guy who runs my operations department, Leo Mendez," Blake continued. "He's like my right-hand man. Keeps the wheels spinning at the company. He is great at keeping Transformation's name in the media, and—"

"*Blake,*" Mona interrupted. "I didn't come here to talk about Transformation Cosmetics. I'm here to discuss Olivia, and what you think may have happened to her."

He cleared his throat, staring across the table at Mona while rubbing his hands together. She could've sworn there was a glimmer of irritation in his eyes.

"My apologies," he said. "I just get carried away by the good that my company is doing. It's a nice distraction from everything else that's going on."

"You mean the fact that your wife is missing? I'd think that finding her would be your number one priority. Not indulging in things to take your mind off of it."

"You're right." Blake's face began to redden as he fiddled with his mustache. "And it is. You said you wanted to catch up. So I was just explaining what I've got going on and why I have to cut this meeting short.

I hope you didn't take it as me wanting CNB News to cover the toy drive or anything."

When he raised his eyebrows expectantly, Mona realized that's exactly what he was doing.

Mona sat straight up in her chair, struggling to maintain her composure.

"Considering the fact that your wife is missing, I seriously doubt that CNB's viewers would be interested in your company's toy drive. They would, however, want to hear your take on Olivia's disappearance. Would you be willing to do an on-air interview with me to discuss that?"

Blake turned in his seat, crossing his legs and propping his folded hands over his knee.

Mona noticed that he wasn't wearing his wedding ring.

"I would give it some thought," he told her.

She'd heard that wavering tone time and time again. It reeked of insincerity.

"But," Blake continued, "I'd have to discuss the potential interview with my attorney before I agree to something like that."

"Oh? So you've hired an attorney?"

"Of course I have. I'd be a fool not to." Blake paused, running his hand down his impeccably pressed slacks. "Listen, Mona, I know you think I had something to do with Olivia's disappearance. But I can assure you that I didn't."

"Can you?"

Mona pulled a red leather-bound notebook from her purse and slid the slim silver ink pen from its holder. She flipped to a blank page, then stared up at Blake, tapping the pen against the table.

"How was Olivia's mood the day that she went missing? Was she sad? Stressed? Seemingly normal?"

He paused, his jaws clenching as he turned toward the window. "I didn't actually see Olivia the day she went missing."

"What do you mean? You didn't see her that morning before you two left for work?"

"No. I didn't."

"But how could you—"

Mona stopped abruptly. She studied the crumpled look of guilt on Blake's face.

"So I'm assuming you weren't home that morning?" she probed.

"No… I wasn't."

Mona took a deep breath. She grabbed her cup of maple hot chocolate and took a long sip.

"Did Olivia know you were having an affair?" she boldly asked.

Which would've been the perfect motive for you to harm her if you did, she was tempted to add.

"I don't believe so. If she did, she never questioned me about it."

"Of course not. Olivia's always been too sweet and passive for her own good."

Blake eyed Mona, appearing as though he wanted to refute her statement. But before he could, his cell phone rang.

"Could you please excuse me?"

He didn't wait for Mona to respond before picking up the call.

"This is Blake. Yes, I'm still over at Kimmy's. Okay, I'll be there in a few minutes."

Blake disconnected the call, then stood up.

"Sorry to cut our little chat short, but the PR consultant has arrived at my office. I need to get back for our meeting."

"There's a lot more I'd like to discuss with you, Blake. You could have information that will help us find Olivia."

"Have you talked to her brother yet?"

"No. Why would I? Olivia and Oliver aren't close. Never have been."

"Yeah, well, he may know more than you think."

Mona slowly leaned into the table. "What makes you say that? Has he been acting strange around the office?"

"I wouldn't know. I fired him two months ago."

"Really? Why?"

"Because of that hot temper of his. He throws tantrums like a two-year-old child. And I blame his parents for that. Thanks to all their coddling, Oliver is out of control."

"What exactly did he do to get fired?" Mona asked.

"He snapped on Leo, who was his boss, mind you, one too many times. During the last incident, Oliver got mad because Leo asked him to recount a shipment of boxes. The confrontation got so heated that Oliver swung a fist at Leo. That was it for me. I don't care if Oliver is my brother-in-law. He needs help. I'm talking serious anger management."

"Hmm, sounds like he's gotten worse since college."

"Oh, trust me," Blake quipped, "he has. And you know how jealous he is of Olivia. If he could get that angry over a warehouse delivery, imagine what his resentment toward her could drive him to do."

Mona studied Blake's stern expression. She wondered whether he really believed Oliver was involved in Olivia's disappearance, or if he was trying to pin it on him to take the heat off himself.

"Listen, I know you're really busy," Mona said, "especially during this time of the year. But I also know how important finding Olivia is to you."

She paused, waiting for Blake to agree with her. But he just stood there, staring back at her blankly.

Several moments passed before he finally spoke up.

"Yeah, yeah," he muttered. "Of course."

"Well, I would really like to sit down and talk with you again. And if possible, conduct that interview live on air—"

Mona was once again interrupted by the ringing of Blake's cell phone.

"That's Leo again," he told her. "I've gotta get back to the office. I'll reconnect with you soon. And don't forget," Blake reminded her as he headed toward the exit, "reach out to Oliver and see what he has to say for himself!"

Mona watched as Blake spun around and jogged out of the shop. She immediately grabbed her phone and composed a text message to Dillon.

Just wrapped up the meeting with Blake. Are you available to talk? Got a lot to catch you up on.

Dillon responded within seconds.

Can we catch up early this evening? I've got my hands full down here at the station.

Sure, Mona wrote back. Just call me whenever you're free.

She closed out the text message thread and opened her Instagram account. Mona searched for Oliver's page, which he posted to regularly with various celebrity conspiracy theories.

She found it and clicked on the most recent post.

Think your favorite celebrity is dead? Well think again! Many of our beloved entertainers INTENTIONALLY disappeared in order to escape the evils of HOLLYWOOD! Swipe left to check out the celebs I KNOW are still alive!

"This man is ridiculous," Mona mumbled.

She tapped the direct message link and began composing a private message to Oliver.

Hi there. Mona Avery here. It's been a while. I hope you're well. I'm in town covering Olivia's disappearance and would love to get together and talk with you. Please reach out and let me know if you're up for it, and if so, when. Hope to hear from you soon…

She sent the message, then sighed deeply, disappointed in the outcome of her meeting with Blake. It was too short and he was too vague. While she had gotten him to admit to having an affair, that wasn't much of a secret to many in Lake Landry.

She drained her cup of maple hot chocolate and checked her emails. After responding to a few, she opened Instagram again and checked her direct messages. No response from Oliver yet.

"Ugh," she sighed, worried that she wouldn't hear back from him.

Mona gathered her things and headed toward the exit. On the way out, she saw Kimmy standing behind the counter, filling a tray with wreath-shaped tea cakes.

"Great seeing you, Kimmy," she called out, smiling at the woman known as Lake Landry's surrogate grandmother. "The holiday hot chocolate special was delicious."

"You're so welcome, Mona! It was wonderful seeing you, too. And hey, *please* find out what happened to our girl."

"I will. I promise."

A few customers standing at the counter turned toward her. Before they could get started with a slew of questions, she hurried out the door.

"WHAT ARE YOU DOING?" Mona asked herself. "What exactly are you doing?"

She glanced out the window. No one was around. No cars were parked along the curbs, nor were they driving down the desolate road.

Mona had once again returned to the Beechtree neighborhood where Olivia had supposedly gone missing. The last time she'd visited the area, it was pitch-black. Now it was the middle of the day, and sunlight shone down on the bleak, deserted area. This meant she could get a better look at the alleged crime scene and hopefully find evidence that law enforcement overlooked.

Come on, Mona, she thought. *You promised Dillon you wouldn't do this...*

But Dillon was tied up at the station, and she was itching to do something that would help move the investigation forward.

Mona pulled over near the body of water. She turned off the engine and stepped out of the car.

A strong gust of wind whipped past her and slammed the door shut. She looked up at the sky. The bright sun had suddenly been concealed by looming gray clouds.

"Please don't rain," she groaned, realizing she hadn't packed an umbrella.

Mona contemplated getting back inside the car, heading to the inn and waiting for Dillon to contact her.

But that just isn't who you are, the headstrong journalist reminded herself before setting off toward the body of water.

She stared down at her cream outfit and tan suede ankle boots.

"The least you could've done is gone back and changed," she muttered to herself.

But it was too late now. Adrenaline was pumping through her veins. She was officially in investigative mode.

Mona trudged through the damp marsh. Her eyes darted around the field, focusing on every patch of grass and lump of mud around her.

She stopped abruptly when she noticed an obscure-looking pile of branches up ahead.

A pang of terror thumped in the pit of her stomach. The thought of finding Olivia's body flashed through her mind.

Stop that! she thought, raising her hands to her temples and squeezing tightly. *Stop it now!*

The words reverberated through Mona's head like a shrill scream. She couldn't believe her mind had gone there. She was used to having more control of herself during these investigations. But this case was different. It was personal.

Nevertheless, Mona reminded herself she had to keep calm and remain in work mode.

Toughen up. Focus on the facts. Keep it business.

She took a deep breath and approached the pile of branches. She began sifting through them, bracing herself for what may come. A shoe. A lock of hair. A piece of clothing. Anything that would indicate that Olivia may have met her demise out there near the water.

But she reached the bottom of the pile without finding anything.

"Thank goodness," Mona breathed, wiping her damp forehead before forging ahead.

She continued searching for any bits of evidence or disturbed areas of land. Cleared marsh. A gathering of leaves. A pile of rocks. Nothing appeared out of place.

When she reached the edge of the water, Mona's cell phone buzzed. She pulled it out and tapped the notification. A text message appeared. It had been sent from an unknown number.

LEAVE LAKE LANDRY!

Mona's hand trembled as she quickly shoved the phone back inside her pocket.

"Ignore it," she told herself. "Don't give in to the threats. Stay focused on finding Olivia."

Mona closed her eyes and took a deep breath. She stared down at the gravel-filled soil. A surge of energy shot up her calves. She willed the land to speak to her. Show her a sign of something. *Anything.* Footprints. An earring. A glass test tube Olivia may have been using to collect water samples.

But there was nothing.

Mona continued along the water's edge. She pulled her phone back out and began filming a video of the area. If she couldn't find anything now, maybe she could zoom in on the video and something would pop out at her that she'd missed.

Just when Mona laid eyes on a silver chain twisted within the dirt, she heard tree branches rustling behind her.

She spun around. Bald cypress tree leaves swayed erratically in the wind. Mona squinted her eyes, studying the bright green foliage.

Within the brush, she could've sworn she'd seen a blur of blackness fumbling about.

"What in the…?"

She turned her phone toward the image and continued filming. A sharp tingling crept through her fingertips, making its way up her arms, then quickly washing over her entire body.

Mona knew the sensation all too well. It was a feeling of regret.

I shouldn't have come here…

"Hey!" she yelled, "who's out there?"

No one responded. But as she continued to observe the brush, Mona noticed a shadowy figure. And then, a flash of silver metal.

She gasped.

A gun?

Mona's mouth fell open. She almost let out a scream before quickly tightening her lips. Despite her hand's violent trembling, she continued filming the area.

"I can see you!" she shouted. "And I'm filming you!"

Slowly backing away from the water, she prayed that her heels wouldn't catch on the uneven earth. She waited for whomever was loitering in the brush to step forward or run away. Neither happened.

Fear sucked the breath from Mona's lungs. She tried to inhale but felt as though she were being suffocated.

She contemplated making a run for it. Then Mona remembered the chain buried in the dirt.

You've got to get that necklace!

She kept her phone's camera rolling while slowly inching her way back toward the chain. She kept her head up while glancing down at the ground.

Found it!

Just as she bent her knees and reached for it, Mona's heel sank down into a mudhole.

She fell backward, crashing onto the dank wetland.

Dammit!

As she struggled to stand up, tree limbs once again crackled in the distance.

Mona froze, expecting someone to jump out and rush her.

She watched in horror as a pair of black leather gloves pulled the branches apart.

Just when a black combat boot appeared, the shrill sound of a car horn blew in the distance.

The combat boot paused. It quickly disappeared back into the brush along with the black leather gloves.

A wave of relief ripped through Mona's chest. She dug her fingers into the dirt, pulling her heels up while scrambling to get on her feet. Her legs shook as she steadied herself.

She studied the wooded area where the lurker stood,

hoping he'd fled the scene. When Mona felt safe enough to make a run for it, she darted toward her car.

Wait! The necklace!

She stopped abruptly, emitting a dread-filled whimper. She spun around, praying that the man was gone while retracing her steps.

"Where is it? Where is it?" she hissed.

Mona stared down at the ground, seeing double as her eyes filled with tears. Her head twisted frantically while searching for the silver chain amid tall blades of grass, scatters of pebbles and pockets of water.

Come on...come on...where is it?

A stifling panic filled Mona's chest at the thought of the lurker reappearing.

But despite her fear, she refused to leave until she found the chain.

She hobbled closer toward the water's edge, stumbling through the muddy gravel. Her boots were covered in dirt. She bent down and clawed at the soil, her frustration growing.

She wondered if Olivia felt the same level of fear right before she went missing. In that moment, Mona felt more connected to her friend than ever.

I am going to find you, Olivia...

A shrill car horn once again filled the air. Mona jumped at the startling sound. She contemplated leaving the necklace behind and coming back for it tomorrow with backup.

Just when she turned to rush off, a flash of metal caught her eye.

It was the necklace.

She quickly pulled a tissue from her pocket and

grabbed the chain, careful not to taint it with her fin-gerprints.

Once she'd slipped it securely inside her pocket, Mona ran toward the street.

Boom!

She stopped in her tracks at the sound of a loud ex-plosion.

Oh no. Oh no.

Mona looked up as flames blazed through the air. She stumbled to the curb.

Her car had been set on fire. The words *GET OUT* were spray-painted across the hood.

"What the…?" Mona uttered, shocked at the sight.

She caught a glimpse of a man dressed in all black, charging into the woods.

Mona slowly backed away from the scene, then spun around and took off running toward a nearby thrift store.

"Somebody help me!"

Chapter Four

Dillon pulled up in front of the inn and strolled inside the lobby. He glanced around the cozy French-themed room, admiring the colorful Christmas decorations while searching for Mona.

He walked past a group of chatty, overly made-up women. They squealed loudly while ranting over a new eyeshadow palette that had launched just in time for the holidays.

Dillon chuckled at their enthusiasm. Their joyful demeanor, along with the festive cream-colored berry wreaths hanging from the walls, gold garland lining the railings, and Fraser fir Christmas tree standing in the corner of the room, made for quite a merry atmosphere.

He glanced over toward the fireplace. There, sitting underneath a row of white satin stockings hanging from the mantel, was Mona.

Dillon felt an abrupt pounding inside his chest. He cleared his throat, rubbing his neck before walking toward her.

Even dressed in a white tank and navy blue leggings, Mona looked beautiful. Her head was propped against the back of an emerald green Louis XVI–style chair. She was staring up at the wood beams adorning the inn's vaulted ceiling.

As he got closer, Dillon noticed Mona's delicate face was plagued with a melancholy expression.

He was hit with a sense of alarm.

"Detective Reed!" he heard someone call out.

He turned and waved at Evelyn, The Bayou Inn's manager.

"Hey, Ev. How are you?"

"I'm great! It's so good to see you!"

The short, stout woman giggled while running her fingers through her chestnut brown pixie haircut. She pressed her thin lips together, spreading burgundy-stained gloss even farther outside of her lip line.

"Good to see you, too," he replied, smiling graciously at her blatant flirting.

Dillon turned his attention back to Mona. She was staring directly at him.

They locked eyes. For a few brief moments, it felt as though everything around them had stopped.

He inhaled, his breath catching in his throat as he sauntered toward her.

"Hello, Mona," he said, hoping the thumping in his chest didn't resonate in his voice.

Mona sat straight up and placed her cup down onto the coffee table.

"Hey, Dillon. How was your day?"

Dillon tilted his head, observing her rigid demeanor.

"My day was long. And busy. May I?" he asked, pointing over at the chair next to hers.

"Of course. Please, have a seat."

As he sat down, Dillon noticed Mona shifting awkwardly in her chair, now seemingly unable to look directly at him.

"Are you okay?" he asked her.

"I, um, not exactly," she muttered, picking up her cup and staring down at its contents.

Before Dillon could ask why, Evelyn came bouncing over.

"Detective *Reeeed*," she sang while rubbing her hands together. "I know you're always looking out for that waistline of yours, but have you had dinner yet?"

"No, actually. I haven't. And I already know you've probably cooked up something spectacular tonight."

"I most certainly have. Would you like to hear about it?"

"I most certainly would," he said.

Dillon glanced over at Mona. He noticed she'd placed her hand over her stomach.

"Hey," he said to her, "are you all right?"

"I'm fine," she replied a bit too quickly. "I'm just feeling a bit under the weather. Evelyn was nice enough to make me a cup of ginger tea in hopes of settling my stomach."

"Oh, okay," he replied, eyeing her suspiciously. He could sense that something wasn't quite right.

"I'm so sorry you're not feeling good, dear," Evelyn chimed in. "I hate that you're gonna miss out on my spicy Cajun chili and creole corn bread. I added extra jalapeno peppers and cheddar cheese to give it that good ole Bayou Inn *oomph*."

"Ooh," Mona moaned, placing her hand over her forehead and closing her eyes.

Dillon could see that her reaction had hurt Evelyn's feelings.

"I'll tell you what, Ev," he said. "If it's not too much trouble, why don't you bring me a cup of eggnog hot chocolate for now. And I'll take a bowl of chili, side of corn bread and a few peppermint beignets to go."

"That wouldn't be any trouble at all. Mona, can I get you anything else other than the tea? A glass of ice water? A few crackers or a piece of toast?"

"Thanks, but I'm fine for now."

"Okay, hon. Just let me know if you change your mind. Detective Reed, I'll be right back with that hot chocolate and will put in the to-go order for you."

"I appreciate it."

Dillon watched as Evelyn hurried off. As soon as she was out of earshot, he turned to Mona.

"Hey, what's going on with you?"

"I just had a really rough day," she sighed.

"So I'm guessing your conversation with Blake didn't go very well?"

Mona hesitated, pulling at a piece of thread hanging from her leggings.

"I guess you could say that."

"Do you wanna talk about it? Maybe put our heads together and decipher whatever information you were able to pull out of him?"

She remained silent, still staring down at her lap. When Dillon noticed her eyes welling up with tears, he knew there was something she wasn't telling him.

He reached over and gently placed his hand over hers.

"Hey," he said, "I know this isn't easy for you. Your friend has gone missing. That's tough. And even though you and Blake don't have the best relationship, you've known him for a long time. The thought of him harming someone you care about hurts. But that's why you're here. To help find out what happened to Olivia. So hang in there. Together, you and I are going to solve this case. Okay?"

"Okay," Mona whispered.

Dillon's detective instincts kicked in. He sensed that there was something more going on than what Mona was telling him.

But his interrogative skills told him to back off. Whatever she was holding in, he knew she wasn't ready to discuss it.

"Well I've got some pretty interesting news to share with you," he told her.

She finally looked up at him. "You do?"

When her damp, doe-like eyes connected with his, Dillon felt the urge to lean over and kiss her.

Reel it in, man...

The moment was interrupted when Evelyn came over and handed him a cup of hot chocolate.

"Here you go, Detective Reed. I just whipped up a fresh batch for you."

"Thank you so much."

When Evelyn just stood there, running her hands down the front of her frilly red-and-white apron, Dillon realized she was waiting for him to take a sip. He immediately placed the mug to his lips and tasted the sweet drink.

"Mmm, this is absolutely delicious," he told her.

Evelyn leaned back and rapidly clapped her hands. "Ooh, I just love hearing that! Thank you!"

"You're welcome."

An awkward silence fell over the threesome. After a few moments, Evelyn pulled a stack of beverage napkins decorated with boughs of holly from her pocket. She placed them down onto the coffee table, then cleared her throat.

"Well, if there's anything else I can get for you two, just give me a holler. And, Detective, I'll bring out your to-go order whenever you're ready to go!"

"Thanks again, Ev," he chuckled.

Both Mona and Dillon watched as she practically skipped back to the kitchen.

"Someone's got a little crush on you," Mona teased.

"Nah, I'm just the new guy in town. When the next one moves here, Evelyn will forget all about me."

"I doubt that. You're not the forgettable type."

Dillon's head shot up so quickly that he almost spilled his hot chocolate. He eyed Mona intently, wondering whether she was flirting with him.

"So," she continued, "what is it that you were going to tell me?"

"I received a call from Olivia's mother this afternoon. She shared some pretty interesting information with me."

"Really? I've been trying to get by there to see the Whitmans. But we just can't seem to coordinate our schedules. I honestly think they're hesitant to speak with me because of my ties to the media. Like you, they're probably convinced my involvement will turn this case into a media circus."

"Correction," Dillon pointed out, "I *used* to think that. But I don't anymore. Anyway, I'll see what I can do to get you in front of them. I'm sure they trust you enough to know that you wouldn't say or do anything to jeopardize the investigation."

Mona gripped the mug and gulped her tea so quickly that she began to choke.

"Are you okay?" he asked, hopping up and patting her back.

"I—I'm fine," she insisted, waving her hand. "Go ahead. Continue with what you were saying."

Dillon slowly sat back down. He waited until her coughing fit was over before continuing.

"So in addition to speaking with Mrs. Whitman today, I also met with Chief Boyer. Between the two of them, I discovered a couple of details about this case that were missing from Olivia's file."

"Really? Such as?"

"First of all, Blake wasn't the one who reported Olivia missing. Mrs. Whitman did. On top of that, Olivia had been gone for an entire *week* before the call came in."

Mona's eyes widened as they darted around the room.

"Are you serious? Those are two extremely important facts that could change the course of this investigation."

"They most certainly could. As you know, the first forty-eight hours into an investigation are the most critical. We lost a lot of precious time during the week Olivia went missing. Law enforcement could've been fresh on the assailant's trail, gathering clues and crucial evidence, and collecting video surveillance that's probably been taped over by now. Not to mention witnesses who may have been willing to come forward back then have since disappeared."

Mona groaned loudly, crossing her arms in front of her.

"But wait," she said. "How is it that Olivia was gone for an entire week before anyone thought to call the police?"

"Well, according to Mrs. Whitman, she and her daughter only talk about once a week. Between Olivia's demanding work hours and her parents' various business and personal endeavors, everybody's extremely busy. So her absence went unnoticed. Everybody thought everybody else was keeping up with her."

"And Blake *certainly* couldn't be counted on to keep up with his wife."

"What do you mean?"

"He was so busy running around with one of his mistresses that he didn't even see Olivia the morning she went missing."

"And I'm assuming you found that out during your meeting with him today?"

Mona paused.

Dillon noticed her eyes had glazed over, as if she were lost in thought.

"*Hello.* Mona? You still there?"

"Oh!" she uttered, grabbing the arms on her chair and sitting straight up. "Yeah, I'm here. Sorry, I just… so, anyway, what were you saying?"

Dillon observed her fidgety behavior. He ran his fingertips down his goatee, growing more concerned with her strange demeanor.

"I was asking if Blake told you he wasn't at home the morning that Olivia went missing."

"Yes. He did."

He waited for her to elaborate. When she didn't, he continued.

"When I spoke with Mrs. Whitman, she told me that

she'd received a call from a friend who works for Sage Insurance. That's the company that issued Olivia's and Blake's life insurance policies. About a month before Olivia's disappearance, Blake met with their agent and upped the amount of her policy."

"Did he up the amount of his, as well?"

"No, he did not."

"Of course he didn't," Mona said, slamming her hands against her thighs. "I can't believe Blake's greedy ass. It's not like his family isn't loaded. Wait, no. Actually, I can believe him. Too much is never enough. That man has always been excessive when it comes to every aspect of his life. From his collection of sports cars to his fancy watches and ridiculously expensive vacations, he's always done the absolute most."

"Yeah, I can see that. During this investigation, I've learned that Blake is all about his powerful, lavish image."

"Period. His image is the only reason he married Olivia. Blake, along with his father and Mr. Whitman, couldn't wait to merge their two families and create this powerful empire."

Dillon sat back and took a long sip of hot chocolate. "I think we can both agree that when it comes to this case, all roads are leading back to Blake. We're gathering a good amount of circumstantial evidence against him. But we still need more. Something solid enough to really pin this on him. I'm hoping we can—"

"Dillon," Mona interrupted, her voice strained. "There's something I need to tell you."

He slid toward the edge of his chair, giving her his undivided attention.

"I'm listening. What's going on?"

She once again diverted her gaze away from him.

"After my meeting with Blake, I went back to the Beechtree area where Olivia was collecting water samples."

Dillon froze, completely dumbfounded. He blinked rapidly, struggling to focus on Mona as if that would help him better understand what she'd just said.

"Hold on," he said. "You did *what*?"

"I went back to Beechtree this afternoon."

"But...*why?* You and I had an agreement. You promised me that you wouldn't make any more moves without my knowledge, did you not?"

"Yes," Mona croaked, her voice barely a whisper. "I did."

Dillon set his mug down, no longer in the mood for hot chocolate.

A seething anger brewed deep within him. He almost blurted out how this was the reason he didn't want to team up with her in the first place.

"So what happened while you were there? Obviously something went down. I noticed how rattled you were the minute I walked through the door."

Mona pulled a tissue out of her tote bag and placed it on the table.

"The good news is," she began, "I found a necklace buried in the soil near the water source. It may belong to Olivia. Do you think you could take it down to the lab and have it tested for prints?"

Dillon leaned forward, watching while Mona carefully opened the tissue and revealed a silver chain.

"Of course," he replied. "*Wow.* How did you even spot that?"

"A better question is, how did you and your fellow officers miss it?"

He shot Mona a look.

"Careful. Now's not the time for you to get snarky. You're already on thin ice for returning to a possible crime scene without me. You've managed to violate the terms of our partnership before it really even got off the ground."

"You're right. I'm sorry."

Dillon got the attention of the inn's bellhop and asked for a plastic baggie, then turned back to Mona.

"Nevertheless, this was a great find. So thank you. I obviously need to have my crime scene investigators process that Beechtree area again."

"I think that would be a good idea. Hopefully the necklace will produce DNA evidence that'll give us some answers as to who's involved in this."

"That would be ideal," Dillon said. "Because so far, I've been hitting one dead end after another. The people I've questioned. The areas I've searched... It's as if Olivia just vanished into thin air. There's been no activity on her credit cards and bank accounts, no pings on her cell phone, nothing."

Mona pressed her fingertips against her temples.

"That's what is so frustrating about this case. I thought I'd come to town, reconnect with the Whitmans and other townspeople, and get some real leads on what may have happened to Olivia. But no one's talking. It's as if the entire Lake Landry community is afraid to speak on the record."

"But people seem to really trust and like you. Maybe you should start talking to possible witnesses off the record and maintain their anonymity."

"Good idea. It's just more credible when witnesses show their faces and reveal their identity." Mona sighed heavily and slid down in her chair. "Hopefully when I report on that necklace, the community will find that encouraging. It'll be a sign that the investigation's moving forward. You never know. That could lead to someone coming forward with information they may be withholding."

Dillon held up his hand.

"Hold on. You're planning on telling the public about the necklace?"

"Yes. Why?"

"I don't think that's a good idea, Mona. The public doesn't need to know those types of intricate details. It could bring about a lot of chaos. Plus we don't want the suspect to think we're closing in on him just yet. If he's been sloppy and left key evidence behind, I'd like to go in and recover it before he does."

"But *I* collected this evidence. And as a reporter, it's my job to break news and keep the public updated on the status of the investigation."

"I understand that. However, you don't want to compromise our progress, do you? Plus the integrity of this entire operation could be jeopardized as a result of oversharing. Our suspect could even flee Lake Landry before we're able to apprehend him if we reveal too much too soon."

"Fine," Mona muttered, throwing her hands out at her sides. "But you do understand that I'm known for revealing exclusive details that no other journalists have, don't you?"

"I do understand that. Nevertheless, we are not going

to compromise this investigation for the sake of your reputation."

Mona opened her mouth to speak. Dillon quickly continued before she could interject.

"Why don't we change the subject? You mentioned that finding this necklace was the good news. Does that mean you also have bad news?"

He watched as Mona rocked back in her chair. She hunched her shoulders, once again staring down at her lap.

Dillon felt as though she was coming unhinged. She picked up her cup, slowly taking several sips of tea as if she were stalling.

This woman is about to drop a bomb on me...

"While I was at the water source," Mona said, her voice wavering uncontrollably, "I received a threatening text message."

"Really? Saying what?"

"To leave Lake Landry. It was actually similar to a text I received shortly after I began covering this case. But I ignored them both. I refuse to be bullied into quitting this investigation."

"Why didn't you report the initial message to law enforcement?" Dillon asked.

"Because I was afraid you'd use that as ammunition to have me removed from the case."

Before he could refute her claim, Mona continued.

"So, anyway, while I was in Beechtree this afternoon, I decided to film a video of the area while searching for evidence. Right when I saw the necklace buried in the soil, I noticed a shadowy figure lurking in the trees."

Dillon's muscles immediately constricted. His body grew hot underneath his tan leather moto jacket.

Don't say a word, he told himself. *Just hear her out.*

"So the next thing I knew," Mona continued, "a pair of hands covered in black gloves appeared from the brush, then a black combat boot. After that? I'm pretty sure I saw a gun."

He glared at Mona, unable to speak. He was overcome by a wave of nausea. The thought of her being in danger turned his stomach.

Mona paused when the bellhop approached the table and handed Dillon a small plastic bag.

"Thanks," he said, throwing her a stare as he dropped the necklace inside.

As soon as the bellhop was out of earshot, Dillon pointed at Mona.

"Please," he muttered through clenched teeth, "continue."

She drained her cup and took a deep breath, blinking rapidly as if she were fighting back more tears.

"I was torn between retrieving the necklace and getting out of there. Then I thought about Olivia, and how desperate I am to help solve her case. That's what forced me to stay and get that chain."

"So let me get this straight. You put your life on the line for something that probably would've still been there had you just gone back the next day with the safety of law enforcement by your side?"

Mona focused on her fidgeting hands rather than his furious stare. "Well, when you put it that way, I guess it doesn't sound like I made the smartest decision."

"Ya think?"

"And that's, um…that's not all that happened."

He groaned loudly. "What else, Mona?"

"When I got back to my car, I saw that it had been set on fire. And the words *GET OUT* were spray-painted across the hood."

Dillon dropped his head in his hands. "I cannot believe this. You know, at the rate you're going, you won't be alive to help solve this case." He jumped up from his chair. "I can't do this anymore. I *knew* this partnership was a bad idea. And you just confirmed that."

"Dillon, wait. Don't leave. I was just trying to—"

"You gave me your word, then completely went against it," he interrupted, unable to hold back his anger. "You're here in Lake Landry assisting in *my* investigation. Which puts you on *my* watch. Yet you decided to go against me and put yourself in an incredibly dangerous situation. I'm done."

"Dillon! Please don't…"

Mona's voice faded in the background as he stormed toward the door. On the way there, he heard Evelyn call out his name.

"Detective Reed! Don't forget your to-go order!"

She ran up behind him and handed over his dinner.

"Thanks, Ev. How much do I owe you?"

"All the great work you're doing for this town? It's on the house. Have a great night!"

"That's really nice of you. Thank you."

When Dillon reached the door, he paused, glancing over at Mona. She stared back at him. The soft, solemn expression on her face was filled with remorse. It almost turned him around and led him back inside the lobby.

Don't give in to it. You don't need these problems.
Dillon turned around, ignoring the pull in his chest while walking out the door.

Chapter Five

Hey, Oliver, Mona typed. I hope you're doing well in spite of everything that's going on. This is my third time reaching out to you. I'd really love to speak with you about Olivia's disappearance. I'm convinced your input could help solve this case. I hope you'll agree to talk with me. Hope to hear from you soon. ~Mona

She sent the message, then glanced down at the clock on her car's dashboard. It was a few minutes before noon.

Mona took a deep breath and stared out at LLL Water Quality Laboratory. No one had exited the stark, redbrick building in the past thirty minutes.

She leaned forward, struggling to see inside the tinted square windows. Not even a shadow of a figure loomed behind the smoky glass.

A haunting feeling came over her. She eyed the four-story structure, which looked more like a penitentiary than an environmental lab.

Mona tried to shake off the chill. But thoughts of Olivia leaving the building for the last time invaded her mind, worsening her fear.

Where are you, friend? What happened to you?

She glanced down at the clock once again. It was now after twelve.

Mona was hoping to run into Bonnie Young, who was one of Olivia's closest work confidants, on her way to lunch.

She was growing desperate to connect with Olivia's inner circle. Since no one was talking, she'd resorted to staking out potential witnesses.

When another chill swept over Mona, she reached down and turned off the air conditioner. Her hand brushed past her cell phone. She grabbed it, hoping that a missed call or text message from Dillon would appear on the screen.

It didn't.

Mona hadn't heard from Dillon since he'd walked out on her at the inn. She had tried reaching out to him over the past several days, to no avail.

The thought of losing Dillon's trust made Mona sick to her stomach. At this point, he had completely iced her out. She was operating on her own.

You shouldn't have told him what happened out there in Beechtree...

"No," Mona said aloud, immediately pushing the thought out of her mind.

Despite her regrets and the result of her actions, she knew she had done the right thing by reporting the attack.

Chief Boyer had reached out to her the day after the crime took place, letting her know law enforcement was doing all that they could to catch the criminal. But so far, no persons of interest had been named.

During the conversation, Mona was tempted to ask the chief why Dillon hadn't contacted her personally to share that information. But she didn't because she already knew the answer. Plus she wanted to mend the rift between her and Dillon privately, without getting Chief Boyer involved.

"Ugh," Mona groaned, slouching down in her seat.

Her frustration level was at an all-time high. She still couldn't believe that Dillon refused to speak to her. Her live broadcasts weren't generating any new leads. She was anxious to speak with Oliver, who'd so far refused to respond to her messages. The Whitmans still hadn't gotten back to her regarding an interview or even an off-camera conversation. And getting Blake to talk to her again seemed like a lost cause.

"This is not going the way I planned..." Mona groaned.

Her stomach rumbled profusely. She hadn't eaten since the afternoon before. But food was the last thing on her mind.

Mona once again glanced up at the lab's entrance. There was still no sign of Bonnie or anyone else.

"This is a waste of time. I'm outta here."

She turned on the engine, deciding that her time would be better spent back at the inn, planning her next broadcast over a glass of white wine and a bowl of crawfish étouffée.

Just when she put the car in Drive, the door to the lab swung open. A tall, slender woman dressed in baggy blue jeans and an oversize white blouse shuffled down the stairs.

Mona leaned forward, her eyes squinting as she studied the woman.

Is that Bonnie? she asked herself, mentally comparing her to the image she'd seen in Bonnie's bio on LLL's website.

Mona watched as the woman brushed her frizzy red bob away from her face, then slipped on a pair of black cat-eye sunglasses.

As she got closer, Mona realized that it was in fact Bonnie.

She quickly put the car in Park and turned off the engine. She climbed out, following Bonnie as she approached a burgundy minivan.

"Excuse me, Bonnie? Bonnie Young?"

The woman paused, dropping her head while staring at Mona over the top of her sunglasses.

"Yes? I'm Bonnie Young. I'm sorry. Do I know you?"

"My name is Mona Avery. I'm an investigative journalist for CNB News. I'm also a good friend of Olivia Whitman's."

Bonnie's eyes lowered. "Oh…yes. I recognize you now."

"I'm in town covering Olivia's case. And I've teamed up with the Lake Landry PD to assist in the investigation."

"I know. I've been keeping up with your broadcasts. You're doing a great job of bringing awareness to her disappearance."

"Thank you. I've done some pretty extensive research online and saw that you and Olivia work closely together here at the lab. I was hoping you'd be willing to sit down and talk with me. Maybe share some insight into what was going on with Olivia before she went missing."

Bonnie nodded her head, then glanced down at her

watch. "I'm actually heading to a doctor's appointment."

When she hesitated, Mona held her breath, hoping she'd find the time to speak with her.

"But I guess I do have a few minutes to spare."

Yes! Mona thought triumphantly.

Bonnie's eyes darted around the parking lot.

"I don't want anyone to see me out here talking to you, though. Hop in your car and follow me a couple of blocks over. We can talk there."

Mona held her hand to her chest. "I will do that. Thanks, Bonnie."

She rushed back to her car and followed Bonnie out of the lot. They drove toward the quiet residential area located behind the lab, where rows of charming bungalow-style homes stood among lush, manicured lawns.

Bonnie pulled over in front of Rosehill Park. Mona parked behind her, their cars discreetly hidden beneath a row of sweet olive trees.

Mona stared out at the park's lush green lawn, watching as young children chased one another around a water lily pond.

Just as Bonnie jumped out of her van, a gust of wind whipped through her wiry curls. Evergreen leaves and yellow flower petals fell from the trees and dusted the hood of the car. Bonnie looked around frantically, as if worried someone were watching.

Mona could see the fear in her eyes. She quickly unlocked the car door.

Bonnie frantically opened the passenger door before climbing inside.

"Whew," she breathed, vigorously rubbing her hands

over her makeup-free face. "I can't believe I'm actually sitting here with you, discussing Olivia's disappearance."

"Well, I really appreciate you finding the courage to talk to me."

Bonnie's head swiveled from side to side.

"Just making sure no one followed us here," she said before turning to Mona. "Listen, I want to share with you what I know. Or at least what I think I know. But you have to promise me that you'll keep my identity anonymous. I do not want to get caught up with the Carter family. You know how powerful they are. And apparently, dangerous…"

Mona pulled out her phone and began recording the conversation. "You have my word. I will not, under any circumstances, reveal your identity during my reporting."

"Thank you."

Bonnie stared down at her wringing hands. She took a deep breath, then cleared her throat. "Did you know that Blake is having an affair with at least two female employees at Transformation Cosmetics?"

"I've heard that. The main one being with his executive assistant, Ayana."

"That's only half-true. He is having an affair with Ayana, but she's not his main mistress."

"Really? Then who is?"

"Cyndi Porter. His marketing manager."

"Cyndi Porter," Mona muttered.

She opened her cell phone's web browser and searched the name. A photo of a woman who resembled a young Naomi Campbell popped up on the screen.

"Oh wow," Mona said. "She's beautiful. But in all

my research, I've never heard of her. Is she a new employee?"

"She is. According to Olivia, she started working at Transformation a little over two months ago."

"So Olivia knows about her?"

"Olivia knows about everything that goes on in Blake's life," Bonnie quipped. "She just plays like she doesn't. But trust me, the file she was building on that man before she went missing was pretty damning. She was days away from turning it over to a divorce attorney."

"Hmm, interesting. So back to this Cyndi Porter. Where did she come from?"

"Apparently, Blake met her at a beauty convention in Atlanta over the summer. She was there working as an independent makeup artist."

"Wait," Mona interjected, "the woman went from being a makeup artist to a marketing manager at Transformation Cosmetics? That's quite a promotion."

"Well, I guess it helps when you start off by sleeping with the president of the company the same day you meet him. The situation quickly escalated into a full-blown affair. Then things got so hot and heavy that Blake moved her to Lake Landry and handed her the coveted marketing manager position. According to Olivia, Cyndi is giving Transformation's vice president of marketing hell, too."

"Isn't the VP of marketing Lenora King?" Mona asked.

"Yes. And she and Olivia are really good friends."

"I'm guessing Lenora's the one who's been reporting all of Blake's indiscretions back to her?"

"You got it," Bonnie confirmed. "And Olivia would

in turn confide in me. She and I were like work sisters, and—"

Her voice broke. She paused, almost choking when her words caught in her throat.

Mona instinctively reached over and grabbed her hand. Pangs of sympathy filled her chest as she watched Bonnie's eyes fill with tears.

"I understand," Mona whispered. "Olivia was like a sister to me, too."

Bonnie's eyelids lowered. She looked out at the children running through the playground.

"Olivia suspected that Blake was being unfaithful for years," she said quietly. "But she tolerated him. Until Cyndi came along. There was something about that woman that made him lose control. When they began their affair, Blake got sloppy. The town started talking. And Olivia was no longer able to turn a blind eye."

"I can only imagine how hurt and embarrassed she must've been."

"Oh, she was livid. And I'm not sure if she'd shared this with you, but Blake was really pressuring Olivia to have a baby. All he cared about was continuing the Carter legacy. But she refused. There was no way Olivia would've brought a child into that toxic marriage."

Mona felt herself growing hot with anger. She rolled down the window, inhaling the cool air.

"This is *so* frustrating," she spat. "I can't understand why Olivia hadn't filed for divorce and left that vile man a long time ago. She has a great job, plenty of her own money… What was it? What was keeping her in that terrible situation?"

"I think she was hoping he would change. But his affair with Cyndi was the last straw. She'd already begun contacting attorneys. And then, mysteriously, she just up and vanished without a trace."

"I knew things were bad between them," Mona said. "But I had no idea they'd gotten that extreme. I wish I would've known all this before I met with Blake."

"He actually sat down and talked to you? I'm surprised."

"Don't be. He knew what he was doing. I got nothing out of him."

Bonnie snorted sarcastically. "That man is the slickest, most narcissistic human being I have ever encountered."

"That he is. So, let me ask you this. Did you see Olivia the day that she went missing?"

"I did."

"What type of mood was she in? Did she seem worried? Or anxious? Or consumed by what was going on in her personal life?"

"Not at all," Bonnie told her. "She was in a great mood. Almost giddy. The fact that she'd finally decided to leave Blake had her feeling empowered. And I was so happy for her. I couldn't wait to see Olivia shine once she freed herself from that man. But then…"

Bonnie once again became choked up.

"I know," Mona said softly, now struggling to hold herself together. "Don't worry. We're going to get to the bottom of this. Lake Landry's police force is working hard to solve this case. And I'm right there with them."

Mona seethed as the words escaped her lips. She felt a sudden urge to pull up in front of the police station, drag Dillon out and force him to arrest Blake.

"I'm glad to hear that," Bonnie sighed. She glanced down at her watch. "I need to get going before I'm late for my doctor's appointment. Do you have a business card?"

"I do." Mona pulled a card out of her purse and handed it to Bonnie. "Please, feel free to call or text me anytime. And if you think of anything you may have forgotten to tell me, reach out. I don't care how small it may seem. We need all the help we can get."

"I will. Thank you."

"You're welcome. And thank *you*."

Bonnie grabbed the door handle. Before stepping out of the car, she looked around, making sure the coast was clear.

The road was empty. Bonnie climbed out and rushed to her van, climbing in and speeding off just as soon as she turned on the ignition.

"Poor woman…" Mona said to herself.

When she reached down to start the car, her cell phone buzzed. A notification popped up on the screen.

Please let this be Dillon…

But when she picked up the phone, Mona saw that it was a direct message on Instagram.

Oliver!

She frantically entered her password and opened the app.

Come on, Oliver, she thought, waiting for his message to load. *Don't let me down. Let's get this meeting scheduled…*

But when she scanned the message, her hopes were quickly dashed.

Dear Ms. Avery,
Rest assured I have received your messages. With that being said, please understand that I do not wish to

speak with you. I've seen your boastful broadcasts on television. If you, along with the Lake Landry Police Department, are as skilled as you think you are, then you should be able to solve my sister's disappearance without my assistance. I want no part of your investigation. Be well.

Regards,

Oliver Bernard Whitman

Mona's mouth fell open. She reread the message two more times before closing it out and shoving her phone back inside her purse.

"You *jerk*," she muttered through clenched teeth.

Before pulling off, Mona felt compelled to check Oliver's Instagram page. She pulled her phone back out and reopened the app, curious as to whether or not he'd posted about Olivia's disappearance.

She scrolled through his feed. Interestingly enough, there was no mention of his missing sister.

Just as stubborn as he's always been...

"All right," Mona sighed. "Time for some wine and crawfish étouffée."

Right before she closed out the app, Mona noticed a photo of Allgood's Bookstore posted to Oliver's page. The caption read, *FINALLY! AN EVENT WORTH ATTENDING!*

Curious, she clicked on it.

My prayers to the universe have been answered! Conspiracy theorist extraordinaire Michael Graham is coming to Lake Landry to discuss his latest book, THE CONSPIRACY CODES UNLOCKED! Meet me at Allgood's this Saturday at

3:00 p.m. I'll be challenging Mr. Graham with a few theories of my own. Trust me, it'll be interesting to say the least. See you there!

"Yes, you will," Mona said, smiling mischievously.

She took a screenshot of the post and saved it in her phone's file folder. If Oliver didn't want to meet with her, then she'd just coincidentally run into him at the event.

Mona felt her shoulders relax a bit. Today was turning out to be a decent day. She'd received some good intel from Bonnie, and now had a plan to get in front of Oliver. It was progress.

There was just one thing missing. Her partner, Dillon.

Mona tightened her grip on the steering wheel, pulling away from the curb. And then, instinctively, she pressed the voice command button on her touch screen.

"Call Dillon Reed."

Her heartbeat stuttered as the call connected. After four rings, it went to voice mail.

"Dillon, hi. It's Mona. I know we haven't spoken, but, um… I have some new information about Olivia's case that I'd like to share with you. There's also an event coming up that Olivia's brother will be attending. Since he's refusing to talk with me, I figured I'd try speaking to him in person. Maybe, uh, maybe you can come with me."

She paused, swallowing hard as she pressed her fingernails into the steering wheel. She felt as though she was pleading with Dillon. She wasn't used to that, nor was she comfortable with it.

"I really want to help get to the bottom of Olivia's

disappearance, Dillon," Mona continued. "And for the hundredth time, I apologize for going back to Beechtree. Please…give me a call. Thanks."

She disconnected the call and exhaled.

"Come on, Dillon. Do the right thing," she muttered while heading back to the inn.

Chapter Six

"Hey, Detective Reed," Chief Boyer said. "How're things going with the Olivia Whitman case? You and Mona got any new leads?"

Dillon paused in the chief's doorway. He was hoping to sneak out of the station before being noticed by him.

He hadn't told his boss about his falling-out with Mona. Now that she and Dillon had spoken and finally cleared the air, he had no intention of doing so.

"Things are actually going well, sir. I turned that necklace Mona found at the alleged crime scene over to the forensics lab. Since this case is our top priority, the tech is working to get the DNA results back as soon as possible. Oh, and Mona received some interesting new information from one of Olivia's coworkers that was pretty insightful."

"Did she really," the chief stated, a crooked smirk spreading across his chubby face.

Dillon chuckled. He leaned against the doorframe and crossed his arms, bracing himself for his boss's inevitable smack talk.

"Come on," Dillon said, "let's hear it. Get it all out. Go ahead and gloat over my partnership with Mona."

"*Me?* Gloat? Why would I do such a thing? All I'm

gonna say is, teaming up with her hasn't been such a bad thing, now has it?"

If only you knew... Dillon thought.

But he resisted the urge to tell Chief Boyer about how his beloved Mona had gone rogue on him.

"No, sir," he said. "It hasn't been such a bad thing at all. I'm actually heading to an event with her now."

"Really? Is it related to Olivia's investigation?"

"It is. Well, sort of. As you know, Olivia's brother, Oliver, has refused to talk to law enforcement. He's also turned down Mona's numerous requests to meet with her. So we're going to *coincidentally* run into him at a book-signing event he'll be attending. Hopefully he will speak to us once we're face-to-face."

"Interesting plan," Chief Boyer replied. "I hope it works. I really want to know Oliver's thoughts on his sister's disappearance. I've known his family for many years. I still can't believe he won't talk to us."

"Yeah, I'm pretty surprised by that, too. But he does seem a bit strange."

"And reclusive. I'm actually surprised to hear he's even attending a social event." The chief paused, pointing up at Dillon. "Wait, how do you and Mona know he's going to be there?"

"She's been monitoring his Instagram account. According to his latest post, he really wants to meet some conspiracy theory author who'll be at Allgood's Bookstore this afternoon."

The chief propped his elbows up on his desk and slowly shook his head. "You know, as a competent, well-respected detective, I can understand why you were resistant when I initially brought Mona on board to help out with this investigation. But you have to admit, she's good. And resourceful. She's able to move through Lake Landry and connect with the community in ways that law enforcement can't. I really do think she's going to help us solve this case."

"I believe you may be right, Chief. And on that note, I'd better get out of here. I have to stop by The Bayou Inn to pick her up on the way to the signing."

"All right. I'm expecting a full report on that new intel Mona received from Olivia's coworker as well as a recap on this book event."

"You'll have that report on your desk first thing in the morning."

"Great. And good luck trying to get anything out of Oliver."

"Thanks," Dillon chuckled. "I have a feeling I'm gonna need it."

As he left the station and walked to his car, he felt a tingling energy creep up his legs. He tried to shake it off. But instead of dissipating, the sensation traveled up his arms and settled in his chest.

And that's when it dawned on him. Dillon was experiencing the thrill of seeing Mona.

Dillon parked in front of the inn and got out of the car. Right before he reached the door, Mona came strolling out.

He stopped in his tracks at the sight of her. She was dressed in a black denim miniskirt and fitted red turtleneck. Her black suede boots clung to her shapely calves.

As she moved in closer, the scent of rose and vanilla wafted from her neck.

Dillon was so mesmerized that he almost lost his balance. He reached behind him and leaned into the passenger door.

"Hello, Detective Reed," Mona murmured, her red-stained lips spreading into an inviting smile. "It's good to see you. Dare I say, I've actually missed you?"

He was struck by her cool, confident demeanor. It urged him to stand straight up and pull himself together.

Dillon straightened the cuffs on his pale blue button-down shirt and ran his damp palms down his dark jeans.

"It's good to see you, too," he said. "And I'm sorry, but did you just say that you've *missed* me?"

"Yes. I did."

Mona approached the car, her arm brushing against Dillon's chest as she waited for him to open the door.

Keep your composure, he told himself.

"Okay," he replied, unable to restrain his flattered grin. "I guess I can admit that I've missed you, too."

"Well, moving forward, I promise to behave myself. So hopefully you won't shut me out again."

"I would appreciate that," Dillon chuckled.

He stepped to the side and opened the passenger door. When Mona climbed inside, he diverted his eyes in an effort to avoid ogling her curvaceous backside.

This is gonna be a long afternoon, he thought before hopping in the car and pulling off.

"I know you told me I can stop apologizing," Mona began, "so I'll just say that I'm glad you finally returned my call. For a minute there, I thought you might report me to Chief Boyer and have him send me packing."

"I thought about it, especially after I saw that the only information you provided in your police report was that someone set your car on fire. I seem to remember far more happening out there in Beechtree that afternoon."

Mona reached over and playfully swiped his arm.

"Nah, I'm kidding," Dillon teased. "I didn't even tell the chief about our disagreement. I knew I'd allow you back in my good graces at some point. I just needed some time to cool off."

"Allow me back in your good graces? Gee, thanks."

"Don't mention it," he quipped as he turned down Jackson Street. "So, did you get everything settled with the rental car's insurance company?"

"I did. And I've already gotten a new rental."

"Good. By the way, we had your original rental processed down at the crime lab. Unfortunately, any DNA evidence that may have been present was destroyed in the fire."

"Ugh," Mona groaned. "Of course it was."

"Don't get discouraged. Trust me, we're going to catch the assailant. Now, let's talk about this whole 'funny running into you here' thing you're trying to pull off with Oliver today. What's your plan? What are you hoping to get out of it?"

"Well, I'm hoping that seeing me in person will pull at his heartstrings a bit. Maybe remind him of the old days, back when we were young and life wasn't so complicated. I don't know if it'll work. But nothing beats a failure but a try."

"Didn't you say you two weren't very fond of each other back in the day?"

"I did," Mona sighed. "But we're adults now. And this is a serious matter. So I'm hoping we can move past all that. I bet you Oliver heard all types of buzz about Blake around Transformation Cosmetics while he was still working there."

"And you think he'd share that with you after making it clear he doesn't wanna talk to you?"

Mona threw her hands in the air.

"Like I said, it's worth a try. At this point, what've we got to lose? I'm convinced Oliver's harboring information that could help solve this case. You know he still lives at home with his parents. Olivia and her mother are extremely close. I can assure you he's overheard plenty about the state of their marriage and problems they're having."

"You're probably right. I just hope you can get him to talk to you. When I told Chief Boyer about the event, he got pretty excited since Oliver hasn't been willing to talk to law enforcement. I promised I'd have a report on his desk first thing in the morning recapping all this new info we're gathering. Or should I say *you're* gathering."

"No. You got it right the first time. *We're* gathering. Partner."

Dillon stopped at a red light and glanced over at Mona. She gave him a reassuring wink.

"Thanks, *partner*," he replied.

That tingling sensation came rushing back.

Keep your cool, big fella...

He made a right turn down Austin Avenue and let up on the accelerator when Allgood's Bookstore came into view.

The busy street was lined with cars. A large group of attendees were making their way inside the store.

"Wow," Dillon said. "Looks like this conspiracy theorist is pretty popular."

Mona turned and stared out the window.

"It does. I just hope Oliver shows up."

"Trust me," he chortled, eyeing the colorfully dressed patrons bouncing around frantically as they entered the store. "From the looks of this crowd, he'll be here."

Dillon pulled into a space near the end of the block. He hopped out and jogged over to the passenger side, opening Mona's door.

When she stepped out of the car, he watched her intently. His grip on the handle tightened when she ran her fingers through her curls, then straightened her skirt before heading toward the store.

"Um, are you coming?" she turned and asked him.

"Oh! Y-yes," he stammered. "Right behind you."

Dillon joined Mona on the sidewalk. As they headed toward the bookstore, he was suddenly hit with a feeling of nostalgia.

He couldn't remember the last time he'd actually been out on a date. It had been more than three years since he'd been in a relationship. He missed that feeling of companionship.

But this isn't a date, he quickly reminded himself.

Nevertheless, their outing certainly felt reminiscent of one.

Stay focused. This woman is here to help solve a case, not fill a void in your personal life...

"Here we are," Mona said, pulling Dillon out of his thoughts as they approached the bookstore.

He stared up at the shop's faded black-and-white sign. The family-owned business had been around for years and was a popular tourist attraction. From rare books on New Orleans culture to vintage costume jewelry once worn by local entertainers, the store was known for its unique finds.

"I've been meaning to stop by this place," Dillon

said, peering through the frosted windows at the books on display. "Seems pretty interesting."

"Oh, you'll be blown away by Allgood's. It's a Lake Landry staple. Glad I was able to help you knock an item off your bucket list."

"Yeah, me, too," he murmured.

He held the heavy wooden door open for Mona and followed her inside. The small, stuffy establishment was packed with an eclectic crowd. Dark wooden shelves lining the walls were filled with rows of books, antiques and odd memorabilia.

An older, balding man sat at a table in the front of the store. He was posing for selfies in between signing books for the enthusiastic fans. His wide grin revealed crooked, yellow-stained teeth. Wiry patches of gray hairs were scattered across his scalp and jawline. His tattered beige tweed blazer had seen better days.

Considering the man's prestigious best-seller status, he wasn't what Dillon had expected.

"That must be the author, Michael Graham," Mona said, pointing toward the table. "He definitely seems... different."

"I agree."

Dillon watched as the author pushed his thick black bifocal glasses up the bridge of his long nose while handing a book to a customer.

"You're wrong, young man!" Michael boomed. "Plain and simple. *Wrong.*"

"No, *you're* wrong!" someone shouted back. "I have proof that all these A-list celebrities who claim to be dead are still alive. *Government* proof!"

"Ha! Sure you do. I'd love to see it."

Dillon craned his neck, peering through the crowd,

trying to catch a glimpse of whom the author was arguing with. When he saw a man step up to the table and lean in closer to the author, Mona grabbed his arm.

"Hey!" she whispered. "There he is. That's Oliver up there fussing with Michael."

"*Humph*. Figures."

Dillon eyed Oliver, whose wild, wavy hair had been pulled back into a messy ponytail. His pale complexion appeared sallow and blotchy. He was wearing a black graphic T-shirt with ripped skinny jeans and white laceless sneakers.

Mona leaned over and whispered in Dillon's ear.

"Oliver looks bad. I remember back when his hazel eyes used to sparkle. Now they just look dull and vacant. And from the looks of those bags underneath them, he hasn't slept in days."

"Yeah, he does look pretty rough," Dillon agreed, forcing himself to focus on Mona's words rather than her lips being so close to his ear. "He appears to be the complete opposite of Olivia. You would never know he comes from such a wealthy family."

A man who appeared to be a store employee approached Oliver and placed his hand on his shoulder.

"Okay, Mr. Whitman," the man told him. "There will be plenty of time for questions after Mr. Graham is done signing books. Let's be respectful and allow other customers a chance to meet the author."

Oliver jerked his arm, forcing the employee's hand off him before pointing down at Michael. "We're not done with this conversation. So don't think you're off the hook. You're gonna hear me out on this."

"Wow," Mona breathed. "He is so irrational."

"Yes, he is. Do you still think it's a good idea to approach him here?"

"Absolutely. It's now or never. Maybe seeing me will make him think I'm interested in all this madness, too. He'll let his guard down, and I can try to get some information out of him about Olivia."

"Good luck with that," Dillon said, watching as Oliver continued to make a spectacle of himself while customers looked on.

"Let's get in line and grab a book," Mona suggested. "I'll let Oliver notice me rather than approaching him first. That way our encounter will seem more natural and coincidental."

"Good idea. I'll follow your lead."

Dillon walked behind Mona as she joined the crowd. He discreetly kept an eye on Oliver, who was now holding court with a group of people over in the corner.

"No!" Oliver yelled. "He did not die in a car crash. His bandmates decided to replace him after they gained international fame. They were worried his drug habit would ruin their reputation. Trust me, that man is still alive. He lives near the Baltic Sea. And I'm here to prove that to Michael today!"

"Do you hear this man?" Mona asked. "He needs to pipe down and stop harassing these people."

"Yeah, he seems to have quite a temper. It's pretty obvious why he got fired from Transformation Cosmetics."

"Can you imagine the rants he probably went on with his coworkers? I bet he had a slew of theories about what was really going on within the company."

Dillon nodded his head. "And within his sister's marriage, too."

"Good point."

As Mona and Dillon reached the front of the line, he noticed Oliver glance over at them.

"Don't look now," he whispered to Mona, "but I think we've been spotted."

"I noticed. Just play it cool."

She and Dillon approached the table. Mona picked up a book while he pulled out his cell phone.

"Mr. Graham," she gushed, "it's such a pleasure to meet you. I am a huge fan."

The author sat back in his chair and ogled Mona from head to toe.

"Well, well, well," he began, "I can certainly say the same, Ms. Avery. I'm a regular viewer of your broadcasts. 'If you see something, say something.' Isn't that your signature sign-off?"

"It most certainly is."

Dillon looked on amusingly, almost bursting out laughing when Michael licked his thin, cracked lips.

While the author and Mona continued bantering, Dillon peeked over at the corner.

Oliver was watching Mona and Michael curiously. His feet shuffled back and forth as he tapped his fingertips against his forehead.

"Here," Michael said, reaching out and taking his book from Mona's hands. "Let me sign that for you. And I'd be happy to take a photo with you, if you'd like."

"Sure, I'd love that. Thank you."

"I can give you my cell phone number, too," Michael continued, "so you can text that picture to me after we take it. Maybe we can snap a few, then look them over while we discuss my book at dinner tonight?"

Before Mona could respond, Dillon stepped in and cleared his throat.

"Are you two ready for that photo?" he asked, throwing the author a look before holding up his cell phone.

Michael glanced at him, then over at Mona. A red veil of embarrassment covered his face.

"Oh…my, uh—my apologies," he sputtered. "I didn't realize you were here with someone."

"No worries," Mona replied cheerily. She smiled coolly for the camera as Dillon snapped their picture.

"I'll just make this out to Mona Avery," the author croaked, his head now buried in the book.

"I appreciate that, Michael. It was very nice meeting you."

"You, as well," he muttered. *"Next!"*

Dillon followed Mona as she strolled past the table.

"Should we grab a little wine and cheese?" she asked.

He realized that Oliver was standing near the hors d'oeuvres station.

"Sure, sounds good."

Mona approached the table and grabbed two plastic cups of red wine without looking in Oliver's direction. She handed one to Dillon.

Through the corner of his eye, he could see Oliver watching their every move.

"Does he see us?" Mona muttered.

"He does. And it looks like he's heading our way."

"All right," she replied, the excitement in her voice apparent. "It's showtime."

Just as Mona and Dillon turned away from the table and faced the crowd, Oliver walked up.

"Are my eyes deceiving me," he scoffed, "or is Mona Avery actually at a conspiracy theory book signing?"

"Your eyes are not deceiving you," she replied smoothly. "Hello, Oliver."

"What's up, Mona? I'm surprised to see a bougie, semi-famous journalist such as yourself at an event like this. What are you doing here? Stalking me?"

"*Stalking* you?" Mona shot back. "Of course not. I didn't even know you'd be here."

"*Sure* you didn't. So you showing up has nothing to do with the post I blasted all over Instagram about the event? Because you were certainly stalking me on that app."

"Don't flatter yourself, Oliver. I just so happen to be a fan of Michael Graham and came to get a signed copy of his book."

Dillon stood there, his head swiveling back and forth between the pair. Oliver remained silent while rocking back on his heels as he glared at Mona. The intensity in his eyes was frightening.

"So," Oliver finally uttered, "you're suddenly a fan of Michael Graham?"

"Not suddenly. But yes, I am."

"Well, what did you think of his last book, *What You Don't Know Can Hurt You*? Particularly the chapter where he broke down the disappearance of—"

"Hello, Oliver," Dillon interrupted, stepping in before Mona's cover was blown. "I'm Detective Reed. I've reached out to you on a few occasions, but we haven't actually met."

"I know who you are," Oliver shot back. He ignored Dillon's extended hand without taking his eyes off Mona.

"So how long have you been in town?" Oliver asked her.

"About two weeks. As you know, I'm here investigating Olivia's disappearance. I've teamed up with Detective Reed, and together we're working really hard to try to find her. Thus far, we've hit a lot of dead ends."

Oliver grabbed a cup of wine from the table and took a long sip.

"*Humph.* How dreadful for the two of you. Maybe Chief Boyer needs a smarter detective on the case."

Dillon took another step forward, preparing to check him. But Mona grabbed his arm before he could speak.

"Oliver," she said, "I really would like to sit down and talk with you. You're obviously a very intelligent and insightful man. I'm sure you're holding on to some invaluable information that could help solve this case."

Dillon abruptly turned toward Mona, shocked by her comments. But when he noticed the sly glimmer in her eyes, he realized she was simply stroking Oliver's ego in hopes of getting a sit-down.

"I'm listening…" Oliver told her, relaxing his shoulders while shuffling his feet.

And it's working, Dillon thought. *This woman is good.*

"You're a deep-thinking man," Mona continued. "I can only imagine the things that must've flown through your mind after hearing all the chatter among your coworkers at Transformation Cosmetics—"

"I don't work there anymore," he declared.

"I know. But when you did, I'm sure the staff was buzzing. And then there's your mom. Surely she's casually mentioned conversations between her and Olivia around the house that you can recall. Maybe about the state of her and Blake's marriage?"

"Maybe…" Oliver mumbled. He drained his cup, then set it down on the table and picked up another.

"This probably isn't the best time and place for us to talk," Mona told him. "So why don't we exchange numbers and arrange a meeting in the next couple of days? How does that sound?"

Oliver chugged the second cup of wine, then pulled out his phone. "I'll need to check my schedule. But yeah, we may be able to work something out. *Maybe.*"

"Awesome," Mona replied.

She took his phone and typed in her number, then sent herself a text message from it so she'd have his.

"Wait," Oliver said, nodding his head toward Dillon in disgust. "If I do agree to meet with you, does he have to come?"

Mona discreetly nudged Dillon's arm, as if she could sense his patience wearing thin.

"Not if you don't want him to."

"Good. Because I don't."

Dillon took a deep breath and turned away from Oliver.

Let it go, he told himself. *Don't say a word. Do not buy a ticket to this clown's circus.*

He raised his cup of wine to his lips. But when he got a whiff of the overly sweet scent of blackberry, he discreetly tossed the cup in the trash.

"Now that we've exchanged contact information," Mona told Oliver, "I'll be in touch to set up that meeting."

He shrugged his shoulders indifferently.

"It's not like I know much," Oliver said. "After all,

I am the black sheep of the Whitman family. And ever since I was *unjustly* fired from Transformation Cosmetics for refusing to bow down to that horrendous Leo Mendez, I've really been on the outs."

"I bet you know more than you think," Mona assured him. "Don't worry. I'll ask all the right questions."

"I'm honestly more interested in discussing Michael Graham's conspiracy theories with you rather than my missing sister. Speaking of which, what do you think of his idea that an extraterrestrial spacecraft really did crash in Roswell, New Mexico, back in 1947—"

"Hey," Dillon interrupted, glancing down at his watch, "we'd better get back down to the police station, Mona. Chief Boyer is expecting us to update him on that, uh…"

"On that report we were working on earlier, right?" Mona chimed in. "Yes. He sure is waiting on us." She tossed her cup of wine in the trash bin, then turned to Oliver. "I'm so glad I bumped into you. I'll be in touch soon."

He threw up a peace sign and slowly backed away from the pair. "Don't get too confident, now. I said I *might* meet with you. Nothing's definite. And hey, if I know something, *maybe* I'll say something," he smirked.

Dillon glanced at Mona. She remained stoic, seemingly unmoved by the taunting jab at her catchphrase.

Before she could respond, Oliver crossed his right foot over his left and spun around dramatically, then marched off.

"What a fool," Dillon muttered. "He doesn't even seem to care that his own sister is missing." He glanced around the room, watching as patrons waved their hands in the air while debating the obscure contents of Michael's book. "This was a complete waste of time."

"No," Mona rebutted, shaking her head emphatically. "It wasn't. Just be patient. By the time I'm done with Oliver, he'll be telling me everything I need to know, plus more. Trust me on that."

"All right, then. I'm glad you're so confident. Because I have no faith in him whatsoever."

"That confidence worked on you, didn't it?" Mona sassed back. "When I first got to town you would barely even speak to me. And look at you now. I've got you calling me your partner and everything."

Dillon leaned back, staring at Mona through the corner of his eye. "You're right," he chuckled, unable to stop gazing at her lush lips. A swirl of arousal shot through his groin as a result of her self-assured swag.

Get your mind right...

He shoved his hands in his pockets and took a deep breath. "I think our work here is done. Would you like to go over and say goodbye to your friend?" he asked, nodding in Michael's direction. "Or should we get out of here before someone questions you about the aliens that the government is housing in some undisclosed underground location?"

"Um, the latter," Mona snickered, swatting Dillon's arm before heading toward the exit.

He followed closely behind her.

Eyes up, he told himself, determined to keep his focus on the case rather than her swaying hips.

Chapter Seven

Hello, Oliver, Mona typed. Texting you once again hoping you'll respond this time. Still looking to conduct an on-air interview with you. We can start with an in-person meeting if you'd like. Looking forward to hearing back and getting on your schedule. Thanks.

She sent the message, then slid her phone across the desk.

"Ugh," Mona groaned, throwing her head back and vigorously rubbing her eyes. She knew solving Olivia's disappearance wouldn't be easy. But she had no idea it would be this frustrating.

She sat straight up and glanced around her hotel room. Clothes were strewn everywhere. She hadn't bothered to sit last night's dinner tray outside the door to be picked up. Her lack of progress in the investigation was weighing so heavily on her that Mona hadn't had the energy to pick up after herself.

But you've gotta keep going...

Mona stared down at her phone and instinctively picked it up. She scrolled through her contacts list in search of Olivia's mother's phone number.

"Being a pest is part of my job," she told herself.

Mona wasn't about to let the fact that the Whitmans

had yet to return her calls deter her from reaching out. She was determined to get them involved in her efforts.

Dillon had explained on numerous occasions that they were hesitant to speak publicly. The Whitmans were convinced that their high profile would attract unwanted attention, false leads and scammers.

Mrs. Whitman trusted that someone would eventually come forward with answers leading them to Olivia.

Mr. Whitman, however, felt differently. He feared the worst. Ever since Olivia went missing, he'd been waiting by the phone for kidnappers to call him demanding ransom money. And he constantly questioned whether or not his daughter was even still alive.

Mona tapped on the Whitmans' phone number and said a silent prayer, hoping they'd pick up this time.

After four rings, the call went to voice mail.

"Dammit," she murmured.

At the sound of a beep, she cleared her throat and put a smile on her face.

"Hello, Mr. and Mrs. Whitman," she said pleasantly. "This is Mona Avery again. I understand that you're both extremely busy and going through a lot right now. But I'm still in town, reporting on Olivia's disappearance and working alongside Detective Reed. I'm hoping to sit down and speak with you. We can do so off camera if you'd prefer. Whatever you're most comfortable with. I just want to help find your daughter."

Mona paused, debating whether or not she should mention the necklace she'd found. That bit of information could prove to the Whitmans that she was making progress in the investigation and worthy of a meeting.

But the sound of Dillon's voice quickly echoed inside her head. She remembered that he didn't want her divulging the details of the case.

Mona had already betrayed him once by going to Beechtree without his knowledge. She didn't want to go against him again.

"So please," she continued, "I hope that you'll return my call. I look forward to hearing from you. Thank you."

Right before she hung up, Mona thought about her run-in with Oliver at the book signing. She didn't know whether mentioning it would give her some leverage. But she figured it was worth a try. The Whitmans were always pleased when their reclusive son actually interacted with other human beings.

"Oh, and by the way, I ran into Oliver at Allgood's Bookstore on Saturday. It was so good seeing him. I'm hoping we can reconnect and catch up. But, anyway, sorry for the long message. Hope to talk to you soon."

Mona disconnected the call. She sighed deeply, taking the last sip of her gingerbread mocha latte. Just as she began to feel ashamed of herself for lying, setting up fake run-ins and withholding information from grieving parents, her cell phone buzzed.

"Please be Mrs. Whitman," she said aloud. "Please be Mrs. Whitman…"

When she grabbed the cell, Dillon's number was displayed on the screen.

Instead of feeling disappointed, a tingling thrill of excitement shot through the pit of her stomach.

What was that? Mona asked herself before picking up the call.

"Hey," she said, her casual tone a total contradiction of the flutters floating inside her chest. "What's up?"

"A lot." Dillon puffed.

"Are you okay? It sounds like you're completely out of breath."

"I am. I just got a call from Martha down at the forensics lab."

Mona jumped up from her chair.

"You did? What'd she say?"

"She got a hit on the necklace. She wants me to come down to the lab to discuss the results."

"Oh my goodness," Mona uttered, her heart beating so rapidly that she could barely breathe. She hurried over to the bed, slipped out of her boy shorts and threw on a pair of beige skinny jeans. "You're taking me with you, right?"

"Of course. I'm on my way to pick you up now."

Mona frantically wiggled her hips as she zipped her pants, then threw on a beige cable-knit off-the-shoulder sweater. She ran over to the mirror and fluffed out her day-old curls, wishing she had time to run her hot wand through them.

"Okay, good. When will you be here?"

"I'm actually turning down the block now. I'll be pulling up in a second."

Mona grabbed her makeup bag, quickly swiping gold gloss across her lips and peach blush over her cheeks.

"I'm on my way down."

"Great. See you in a few."

Mona hung up the phone and tossed it inside her tote bag, along with her notebook and sterling silver pen. She applied another layer of deodorant underneath her arms as she had already begun to sweat, then sprayed citrus perfume on her neck and wrists.

"Wait, what are you doing?" she asked herself. "This is not a date."

She tossed the perfume down onto the bed, rolling her eyes at her own behavior.

Get in work mode. This is business...

Mona slipped on her tan ankle boots and grabbed her bag. She gave herself a brief once-over in the mirror, then ran down to the lobby.

"Hey, Evelyn!" she said while rushing past the front desk.

"Hey! No breakfast today?"

"No, the mocha latte was more than enough. It was delicious."

"Oh good. But you missed out on my famous strawberry-and-creole-cream-cheese crepes."

"Mmm, sounds delicious. I'll be sure to have them next time they're on the menu," Mona told her as she hurried toward the door.

"Sounds good. Well, make sure you're here for dinner tonight. I'm whipping up a batch of my Louisiana beef stew and pecan bread. Hopefully Detective Reed will be able to join you!"

"I'll be here, and I'll see if he's available," Mona chuckled, tickled by Evelyn's crush on Dillon. "See you tonight."

She hurried outside. Dillon was already standing on the passenger side of the car with the door open.

"Hey, thanks for letting me tag along with you," she told him.

"Of course. You're the one who found the necklace. There's no way I would've gone to get those results without you."

Mona paused before sliding inside the car, smiling

at Dillon. While she wasn't easily moved, she'd found his statement touching.

"Thank you, Detective Reed."

The pair gazed at one another. She stood so close to him that the scent of cinnamon candy rolling along his tongue filled her nostrils.

"We'd better get going," Dillon whispered. "Martha is waiting on us."

"Y-yes, we…we'd better," she stammered, feeling as though he'd just broken a hypnotic spell.

The twosome climbed inside the car and Dillon drove off. Mona grabbed the door handle as he whipped around the corner and flew down the street.

She glanced over at him, noticing that he was vigorously running his hand down his goatee. His eyes were darting. His chest was heaving. There was an intensity in his expression that she'd never seen before.

"Are you okay?" she asked him.

"Yeah. I'm good. Just anxious to get the DNA results on that necklace."

"Me, too. Hopefully they'll give us some answers. Or at least lead us in the right direction."

Dillon remained silent as he sped through an orange light and made a sharp left turn down Armstrong Avenue.

When he hit the expressway, Mona pulled out her cell phone, hoping that someone in the Whitman family had gotten back to her.

No new notifications appeared on the screen.

"Unreal…" she moaned.

"What's unreal?"

"I texted Oliver asking if we could get together and talk. He didn't respond. Then I called the Whitmans and left a voice mail, once again asking if they'd meet with me."

"They haven't gotten back to you either?"

"Nope. And I poured it on thick in my message, too. Even mentioned seeing Oliver at the book signing. I was hoping that hearing their son had a conversation with someone outside of his video game headphones would encourage them to talk to me."

"Yeah, well, I already told you where the Whitmans stand. They're trying to keep a low profile through all of this. They don't want the public scrutiny. The family trusts that the police will find their daughter."

"I just wish they understood that I'm an integral part of this investigation, too."

Dillon tapped his turn signal and exited the expressway.

"That you are," he told her. "We wouldn't be heading to the lab right now if it weren't for you. Your contributions to this case have been invaluable. Don't worry. I'm convinced the Whitmans will eventually come around."

"Thanks. I hope so," she replied quietly before turning and staring out the window.

The forensics lab was located in Vincent Parish. It was utilized by law enforcement agencies in several surrounding towns, including Lake Landry.

Businesses and residential homes were few and far between in the rural area. Vast fields of grass lined the long stretch of road leading to the laboratory.

When Dillon stopped at a red light near a row of fast-food restaurants, Mona knew they were almost there.

Her stomach turned nervously. She contemplated the necklace's DNA results.

Please bring back something significant, she thought.

"Hey," Dillon said. "You okay over there? Keep wringing your hands like that and you're gonna rub the skin right off."

Mona stretched her fingers out and rubbed them over her thighs.

"Wow. I didn't even realize I was doing that. I'm fine. Just anxious to find out the results on the necklace."

"Yeah. Same here."

She looked up and saw Volution Technology's dull gray cement building come into view. The sterile structure took up almost half a block. Its thick, narrow windows were tinted, making it impossible to see inside. A few sparse bushes lined the front of the building. The intimidating establishment appeared far from welcoming.

When Dillon pulled into the parking lot, Mona noticed a couple of men dressed in dark suits stepping out of an unmarked car. Their foreheads wrinkled as they clutched file folders while rushing inside the building.

"This place feels more like a prison than a crime lab," Mona said.

"It does. Reminds me of the Louisiana State Penitentiary."

Dillon parked the car and hopped out, running around and throwing open Mona's door.

"You ready to do this?" he asked her.

"I'm ready," she said, taking a deep breath and following him inside.

The pair stopped at the security desk and showed the attendant their IDs.

"Detective Reed and Mona Avery," Dillon said. "We're here to see Martha Scott."

The attendant turned to her computer and entered their names into the system. "Thank you, Detective Reed and Ms. Avery. Please have a seat in the lobby. I will let Martha know that you're here."

"Thanks."

Dillon spun around and placed his hand on the small of Mona's back, leading her toward a row of black plastic chairs.

She gasped slightly, surprised by the rousing feel of his touch. When Mona glanced over at him, Dillon was staring straight ahead. He appeared oblivious to the effect his intimate gesture had on her.

Mona's gait stiffened as her boots clicked loudly along the white speckled tile. She looked around the stark lobby, feeling as though all eyes were on them. But the few people who were scattered around weren't paying any attention to the pair.

"So," Dillon said after they took a seat, "I hope you're not getting discouraged because you haven't heard back from the Whitmans. Just give them some time. They're scared, and still trying to wrap their heads around the fact that their daughter is missing."

"I know," Mona sighed. "But I'm convinced they know something that could help crack this case. I've known them for years. I can get them to open up. I just have to get in front of them."

"And you will. When you do, I have no doubt you'll pull things out of them that no one else could."

"You think so?" Mona asked, surprised that he believed the family would confide in her over him.

"Absolutely. Between your history with the Whitmans and journalistic prowess, you may solve this case all on your own."

"Oh, now you're just trying to win cool points with me," she laughed.

"And? So what if I am?" Dillon asked, glancing over at her with a sly smile.

Mona was seldom at a loss for words. But in that moment, she had no comeback.

She was distracted by the sound of approaching shoe soles squeaking against the tile.

"Detective Reed, so good to see you."

Mona looked up and saw a slender older woman walking toward them. She assumed it was Martha considering she was wearing a white lab coat and holding a file folder.

"Martha, it's good to see you, too," Dillon said, standing up and shaking her hand.

Mona stood up as well, unable to take her eyes off the forensic scientist.

Martha's style was eclectic to say the least. Her hair had been cut into a silver mohawk. Humungous red square eyeglasses covered the top half of her square-shaped face. She was wearing fuzzy purple socks, which were stuffed inside a pair of dingy brown Birkenstocks.

"Martha, I'd like for you to meet Mona Avery."

"Oh, I *know* who Miss Avery is," Martha said, grinning.

She reached out and shook Mona's hand so hard that she felt as though her bones might break.

"I'm a huge fan," Martha continued. "I never miss a broadcast. You are so good at what you do."

"Thank you very much. I appreciate that."

"You're welcome. So, I've got the results back on that necklace. Why don't we go back to my office and discuss my findings?"

"Sounds good," Dillon told her. "Lead the way."

Mona's stomach rumbled as she followed Martha and Dillon down a long white hallway. She bit her tongue, resisting the urge to ask for the results right there on the spot.

When they reached the end of the corridor, Martha led the pair inside her cluttered office.

Her expansive desk was covered with lab tubes, stacks of paper, a microscope and UV lamps.

"Sorry about the mess," Martha said. She pointed to a set of gray tweed chairs. "Please, have a seat."

Mona's thighs quivered as she gripped the chair's arms and slowly sat down. She held her breath, waiting to hear the findings.

Martha appeared to be moving in slow motion. She set the file folder down on the desk and thumbed through the pages.

"So," she finally began, "I was able to pull DNA evidence from the necklace and make a positive identification. Two, actually."

Mona slid to the edge of her seat. Her fingernails dug into the soft wood, chipping away at the chair arms.

When Dillon reached over and gently placed his hand on her arm, she relaxed a bit, appreciative of his unspoken support.

"You know," he said, "I'm surprised the evidence wasn't contaminated despite the necklace being outside in the elements for what I'm assuming may have been several days."

"Same here," Martha replied. "I chalk that up to the universe wanting these results to be found."

The pressure of anticipation pounded inside Mona's head.

"And what were those results?" she blurted out, unable to control herself.

Martha looked over at Mona with a pained expression on her face. Her hands trembled slightly when she picked up the report and slid it across the desk.

"DNA evidence shows that the necklace belongs to Olivia Whitman."

Mona swallowed hard, crossing her arms in front of her tightly. She glanced down at the report, unable to read the words on the paper.

"What exactly did you find?" she whispered.

"There was a hair caught in the necklace's clasp. The follicle that was attached proved it belonged to Olivia. There were also droplets of dried blood collected."

"Olivia's blood?" Dillon asked.

"Yes."

"Oh my God," Mona whispered.

Dillon slid his chair closer to hers and held her hand. She leaned into him. Violent thoughts of what may have happened to Olivia flew through her mind.

Stop it, she told herself. *Stay positive. Do not fall apart.*

"And that's not all," Martha continued. "There was also evidence of fingerprints and skin cells present on the necklace."

"Did you get a hit on who they belong to?" Dillon asked.

"I did. They belong to Olivia. And Blake Carter."

Mona tried to take a deep breath but choked when

the gust of air hit her lungs. She felt Dillon's hand squeeze her shoulder as he tried to make sense of the situation.

"And no one else's DNA was found besides Olivia's and Blake's?" he asked.

"No," Martha said quietly. Her somber tone was filled with remorse. "Just those two."

Mona abruptly turned to Dillon as tears streamed down her face.

"He did it," she insisted. Her voice trembled with pain. "He did it. I *knew* he did it."

"Calm down, Mona," Dillon said soothingly. "Let's not jump to conclusions. It does make sense that Blake's DNA would be on the necklace. He could have given it to her. Or put it on for her."

"But what about the blood evidence?" she pressed. "Why was Olivia's blood on the chain? What happened to my friend?"

"That's what we need to figure out. And this conclusive evidence is a good start. It confirms that Beech-tree was most likely the area where Olivia encountered some sort of danger."

Mona held her hand to her forehead. She felt faint at the thought of Olivia being dead.

"Come on," he said quietly. "Don't get discouraged. I know this case is personal to you. But you've got to remain objective. Stay in investigative mode."

"Easier said than done."

"I know it is. But together we will press on and get to the bottom of Olivia's disappearance. You never know. She could turn up safe and sound tomorrow."

Mona nodded. "You're right. I've got to stay positive."

Martha cleared her throat and closed the file folder.

"I'm so sorry to interrupt you two. But I've got a couple of detectives from Ellis Parish here to meet with me."

She handed Dillon a file and paper bag.

"Here's a copy of my findings as well as the necklace. I really am hoping for a positive outcome in all this. The entire town is. Actually, thanks to Mona's reporting, seems like the whole country is."

Mona took a deep breath and sat straight up in her chair.

"Thank you, Martha. That's the goal. Hopefully bringing awareness to Olivia's disappearance will generate more leads."

As soon as the words were out of her mouth, Mona's cell phone buzzed. She pulled it from her tote and stared down at the screen.

Her stomach dropped when a text message from Mrs. Whitman appeared.

"Thank you again for getting these results back to us so soon," Dillon told Martha before standing up. "I really appreciate it."

"Anytime, Detective Reed."

Mona jumped up from her chair and rushed toward the door.

"Yes, thank you, Martha. It was really nice meeting you."

"Same here. Looking forward to your future broadcasts. Best of luck in solving this case."

"Thanks!"

Mona practically pushed Dillon out of the office.

"I can walk you out if you'd like," Martha called out.

"We're fine," Mona told her. She could feel Dillon

eyeing her curiously as she tapped her security code into her cell phone.

"What is going on?" he asked her. "Are you all right?"

"Yes. I'm more than all right. Mrs. Whitman just texted me."

"She did? What'd she say?"

"I'm about to find out."

Mona pulled Dillon to the side when they reached the lobby and opened the message.

"'Hello, Mona. Thank you for reaching out to us. We've been hesitant to speak with anyone regarding Olivia's disappearance for fear of drawing unwanted attention onto the family. But after receiving your voice mail this morning, Mr. Whitman and I have had a change of heart. We'd like to talk with you, off camera. If you are free this afternoon, you're more than welcome to come by our house. Thank you.'"

"This is good," Dillon said as they headed toward the exit. "After receiving those DNA results, I'm really interested to hear what they have to say."

"I'll confirm that I'm available to meet with them this afternoon and ask if it's okay that I bring you along. I'm sure it will be, but proper etiquette tells me I should get permission."

"I agree. I wonder if Oliver will be there."

"And if he is, I wonder if he'll be willing to talk with us."

Dillon glanced over at Mona, his eyes narrowing skeptically.

"Judging by what I've seen of him so far? I doubt it. But you never know. I guess we'll just have to wait and see. Hey, are you hungry?"

"I am, actually," Mona said. "I skipped breakfast this morning."

"Yeah, me, too. Why don't we go and grab lunch while we wait to hear back from Mrs. Whitman?"

"That sounds good."

Mona and Dillon climbed inside his car in silence. Her body buzzed with a plethora of emotions, from worrying about Olivia to eagerly anticipating her conversation with the Whitmans.

But one thing was for certain. Through it all, she was glad to have Dillon by her side.

Chapter Eight

Dillon sat on one end of the Whitmans' yellow silk couch in the middle of their elaborate great room, sipping a glass of sparkling water. Mona sat beside him, holding a delicate bone china cup filled with mint tea.

Mr. and Mrs. Whitman sat across from the pair in a set of cream silk Victorian-style chairs. She was dressed in a black long-sleeved shift dress and matching pumps. He was wearing a dark blue suit and deep red tie. They both appeared as though they were heading to a funeral.

"Again," Mrs. Whitman said, "my apologies for the delay in getting back to you, Mona. I've just been... we've been so distraught. I'm still in shock that my Olivia is missing."

"So am I, Mrs. Whitman. Trust me, Detective Reed and I are doing all that we can to find her."

Dillon felt his body tensing up. During their lunch, he'd stressed to Mona that she needed to keep the DNA findings of the necklace confidential. He knew that she was emotional and feared that in the moment, while facing Olivia's parents, she'd slip up and mention the results.

Mrs. Whitman sat straight up in her chair, her back rigid. Olivia's disappearance had clearly taken a toll on the regal, attractive older woman. Her light brown complexion appeared washed-out. Newly formed wrinkles of worry lined the corners of her eyes and thin, down-turned lips. Her voluminous brunette hair, which normally hung down her back in a soft cascade of waves, had been pulled back in a severe bun.

The distinguished-looking Mr. Whitman, however, appeared cool and calm. It was obvious he was struggling to remain strong for them both. His short, silverish gray hair was neatly trimmed. His wide-set hazel eyes were clear and alert. He came across ready and willing to share whatever he could to help find his daughter.

When Mona pulled her notepad and pen out of her tote bag, Mrs. Whitman turned to her with fear in her eyes.

"You do understand that this conversation is off-the-record, don't you?" she asked. "Mr. Whitman and I *do not* want the details of our family's personal life being dragged into the public eye."

Dillon shifted in his seat at the shrill tone in her voice.

"Oh yes, of course, Mrs. Whitman," Mona replied. "I'm just taking notes for the sake of the investigation. Whatever we discuss today will absolutely remain confidential."

"Good. Thank you."

The corners of Mrs. Whitman's mouth formed a tight smile. Dillon interpreted it as a silent apology for her abrasiveness.

"The fact that our daughter has gone missing," Mr. Whitman added, "is excruciatingly painful, as I'm sure you can both imagine."

"Absolutely," Dillon told him.

"So I apologize if either Mrs. Whitman or I appear harsh. We're just hurting."

"We understand," Mona empathized. "I hope you know you've got so much support around you."

"Yes, well, not from everyone," Mrs. Whitman rebutted.

"What do you mean?" Dillon asked.

"That damn Blake Carter. The despicable way in which he treated my daughter? I know he had something to do with her disappearance!"

Mr. Whitman reached over and clutched her hand.

"Honey, come on, now. Let's not get ahead of ourselves. We said we weren't going to do that, remember? We promised to be objective and lay out the facts rather than speculate on what we think may be going on in our daughter's marriage."

Mrs. Whitman snatched her hand from her husband's grip.

"Speculate?" she spat. "Oh, this is far from speculation. I heard from my own daughter's mouth how miserable she was in that relationship. Blake is an emotionally abusive philanderer. He's been having affairs with multiple women, shows my daughter no affection unless he wants to have sex with her—"

"Okay, dear," Mr. Whitman interrupted, holding his hand in the air in a bid to quiet her. "Let's maintain some decorum here."

"Decorum…" she sniffed before turning her nose up at her husband. "Believe me, I am working overtime trying to maintain my dignity. But that becomes difficult when discussing such a sorry excuse for a man. If having his cake and eating it, too, were a person, it'd be Blake Carter—"

"Sweetheart, *please*," Mr. Whitman interjected. "Detective Reed and Mona didn't come here for this. They want facts, not the lewd personal details of our daughter's relationship. All that's irrelevant to her disappearance."

Dillon wanted to tell Mr. Whitman that his wife's claims were far from irrelevant. He'd seen numerous cases where infidelity was the motive behind domestic violence incidents. But the pair were so fired up that he decided to keep it to himself for the time being.

Mrs. Whitman glared at her husband before turning to Dillon and Mona.

"As you can see, my husband is in denial. He's also more concerned about preserving the Carter family's upstanding reputation within the community than he is finding our daughter."

"That is *not* true—"

"Detective Reed," Mrs. Whitman continued, ignoring her husband, "I would like for Blake to be questioned as to whether or not he is involved in Olivia's disappearance. Because I for one am convinced that he is."

Dillon scooted to the edge of the couch and cleared his throat. "Well, Blake has been brought down to the station and questioned on more than one occasion. Now, I can't reveal the specifics of the interrogation. But I can tell you that he has a rock-solid alibi on the day that Olivia went missing."

"Of course," Mrs. Whitman sniffed, turning her nose up at Dillon. "That's because he probably hired someone to do his dirty work."

Mr. Whitman's eyes widened as he threw his wife a look of disdain. But this time, he kept quiet.

"Mrs. Whitman," Mona began, "I understand that you don't want to speak publicly about Olivia's disappearance. But in my experience as a journalist, a family's pleas can oftentimes encourage witnesses to come forward with information they'd otherwise keep to themselves. There's something about seeing a parent's pain that motivates people to open up."

"I can attest to that," Dillon chimed in. "Back when I was working on the Baton Rouge police force, I dealt with violent offenders, gang members…all sorts of criminals. Witnesses were afraid to come forward for fear of retaliation. But when the victims' families showed up, pleading with the public for information, tips would start pouring in."

"And when there's a reward attached to these missing person cases," Mona added, "that gives people even more incentive to provide law enforcement with information."

"So wait," Mrs. Whitman said, her sharp tone filled with panic, "has Blake been ruled out?"

"We haven't ruled anyone out," Dillon told her.

Mr. Whitman pressed his hand against his forehead and sighed deeply. "I can just see it now. This entire situation is going to turn into a dog and pony show. The offer of a reward will lead to false tips and con men providing fake information. I watch all those true-crime television shows. I've seen it happen time and time again."

Dillon was surprised when Mrs. Whitman leaned over and gently patted her husband's arm.

"My husband is convinced that whoever kidnapped Olivia is holding her hostage somewhere."

"And if we go public," Mr. Whitman said, "behaving as though we're hurt and weak, this criminal will demand ransom money. Mark my words."

Mrs. Whitman pulled her hand away from her husband. "If that's the case, and Olivia is still alive, I'd give away every dime we have to bring her home."

"As would I," Mr. Whitman shot back. "I just don't want to get scammed out of a fortune without recovering my child."

"Yeah, I don't want us to get scammed out of our fortune either!" Dillon heard someone shout.

The sound of sneaker soles screeching across the foyer's marble floor filled the air. Dillon and Mona spun around simultaneously as Oliver came traipsing into the room.

Mrs. Whitman quickly stood up and rushed over to him.

"Oliver," she hissed, "didn't your father and I tell you to stay upstairs in your bedroom until Mona and Detective Reed left?"

"Yep, you did."

Dillon watched in awe while Oliver brushed past his mother, flopped down onto the love seat next to the couch and propped his shoes on top of the vintage crystal coffee table.

"Oliver!" Mrs. Whitman continued, "please remove your feet from my table!"

He chuckled arrogantly, nibbling at his cuticles. After a minutes-long staredown with his parents, Oliver finally plopped his feet down onto the dark hardwood floor.

Mrs. Whitman's lips tightened. She walked stiffly back to her chair and sat down. Mr. Whitman shook his head. He ignored Oliver while remaining focused on Mona and Dillon.

"As I was saying," Mr. Whitman continued, "I'm just concerned about all of the fraudulent criminals out here who'd try to take advantage of my family. I don't want to appear vulnerable. That's what going public would feel like to me."

Oliver, who was chewing a massive wad of pink bubblegum, threw his head back and blew a huge bubble into the air. All eyes turned to him right before it popped loudly and splattered all over his face.

"Oliver," Mrs. Whitman uttered, "must you? Especially in front of company?"

"Yes. I must," he insisted before turning toward Dillon and Mona. "So, I've been thinking. I may be willing to do that on-air interview."

Dillon looked over at Mr. and Mrs. Whitman. They both stared at their son warily but remained silent.

"Really?" Mona asked hesitantly, her eyes darting back and forth between his parents and him. "What brought on the change of heart?"

"Welp, obviously this investigation has stalled thanks to you and Inspector Gadget over here," he snorted, waving his hand at Dillon.

"*Excuse* me?" Dillon said. "Who do you think you're—"

He paused when he felt Mona's warm touch on his forearm. It immediately silenced him.

"Oliver," Mona continued, "Detective Reed and I are working extremely hard on this case. Keep in mind there are details surrounding the investigation that we're not at liberty to discuss at this time. But trust me when I tell you that things are moving in the right direction."

"Wait," Mrs. Whitman interjected, her eyes brightening with hope. "There are new details that we don't yet know about?"

"Yes," Mona confirmed, "there are. But not enough to make an arrest. We still need all the help we can get from the public. So please, reconsider doing an on-air interview with me."

Oliver hopped up from the love seat and began frantically pacing the floor. "I just said I'd be willing to do an interview. Why am I being ignored?"

"I'm all for you doing an interview," Mona told him. Her gaze shifted toward his parents. "We just need to make sure everyone's on the same page."

Mrs. Whitman stood up again and motioned for her husband to do the same. "Mona, Detective Reed, thank you very much for stopping by. But I think that'll be all for now."

"Oh, so you all are just gonna ice me out like you always do?" Oliver shouted. "I'm sick of being treated like an outcast! Don't forget, I worked with Blake at Transformation Cosmetics. I've seen and heard things that you two know nothing about!"

"Oliver, *please*," Mrs. Whitman begged, walking toward him with her arms outstretched. "Your father and I just want to—"

"I don't wanna hear it!" he yelled, quickly backing away from her. "Keep counting me out. But I'll tell you what. If you and Dad decide to dangle a reward over a witness's head? You may as well write the check out to me now. Because *I'm* gonna be the one who ends up solving this case."

Mrs. Whitman spun around and marched across the room.

"I'll walk you two out," she said to Mona and Dillon while ushering them toward the door.

Mr. Whitman stayed behind with their son, who continued to unravel.

"Mark my words!" Oliver hollered. "It's gonna be *me* who ends up finding out what happened to my sister. *Me!*"

"I am so sorry about all this," Mrs. Whitman breathed.

Dillon was surprised to see her practically jogging to the front door. When she opened it, he noticed tears streaming down her face. She pressed her hand against her cheeks, dabbing away the streaking black mascara.

"No worries, Mrs. Whitman," he told her. "We can only imagine the pain and stress your family is under right now. It's hard to hold it together during times like these."

"And I've known Oliver for years," Mona said, her soothing voice appearing to put Mrs. Whitman at ease. "So I understand his behavior. I know he's hurting. He just has a *strange* way of showing it."

"To put it nicely," Mrs. Whitman replied before chuckling a bit. "Ah, I guess I needed that little laugh."

"I think you did, too." Dillon smiled. "Listen, you have my contact information as well as Mona's. If you think of anything or just want to talk, please don't hesitate to reach out to either of us."

"And not to be overly persistent or anything," Mona added, "but please, just think about doing that interview. As crazy as this may sound, consider allowing Oliver to participate, as well. I know he marches to the beat of a different drummer, but you have to admit, he is engaging. Like he said, he could be integral in solving this case."

Mrs. Whitman remained silent, looking away while crossing her arms in front of her.

"We, uh, we should be leaving," Dillon said as he led Mona out onto the porch. "Thank you again for your time."

"Listen, before you go," Mrs. Whitman said before stepping outside, "can you tell me more about that new evidence you'd mentioned?"

"Unfortunately, we have to keep the details confidential," Dillon replied quietly. "At least for now. But when we're able to, we certainly will."

"I understand. Well, I'll think about what you said regarding the on-air interview. And Mr. Whitman and I will consider allowing Oliver to participate. But he may need some sort of media training in order to do so."

"And that's what I'm here for," Mona said. "I can teach him everything he needs to know before getting in front of the camera. So don't worry. By the time we go live, he'll be a pro."

"A pro?" Mrs. Whitman asked skeptically. "That impulsive son of mine? *Please.* That child will get on air and say anything." She squinted her eyes and stared out at the weeping willow tree standing in the middle of her vast front yard. "But again, I'll think about it. At this point I'm willing to do whatever I can to find my daughter."

"Good," Dillon said. "Again, call us if you need anything."

"I will. Take care."

"You, too," Dillon and Mona replied in unison.

The pair headed to the car, then left the residence in silence.

As Dillon drove back to the inn, he glanced over at Mona. She was looking out at the bleak stretch of grassy swampland, her forehead creased with worry.

"Hey," he said, reaching over and gently nudging her thigh. "Why don't we go out tonight and have a nice dinner? I think we could both use a night off. Maybe talk about something other than this investigation."

"That actually sounds amazing. I definitely need a break from all of this. And as a matter of fact, Evelyn is serving up her Louisiana beef stew and pecan bread tonight at the inn. *And* she extended a special invite just for you."

"Did she?"

"She sure did."

"Well, I guess I can't disappoint Evelyn. Not to mention her beef stew and pecan bread are absolutely superb."

"Yes, they are," Mona agreed. "So, we're on for tonight?"

"We're on for tonight."

Dillon couldn't contain the surge of excitement that erupted inside his chest. It was a sensation he hadn't felt in years.

Stop it, he told himself. *Mona is not into you like that.*

But when he noticed the slight smile on her face, his detective instincts told him otherwise.

Nevertheless, Dillon knew he needed to stay focused

so not to compromise the investigation. Circumstances surrounding the case were growing more dangerous.

Despite his undeniable feelings, he was determined to remain diligent until an arrest was made.

Chapter Nine

Mona sat on a corner stool near the window of Silvia's Speakeasy. She stared out at the dark, desolate street that appeared more like an alleyway. There was no sign of Dillon or Oliver.

She took a sip of her cranberry old-fashioned, then grabbed her cell phone.

Hey, she texted to Dillon. I'm at Silvia's. Been here for almost an hour. Still no sign of Oliver yet. Are you on your way?

Mona sent the message, then swiveled around in her burgundy leather barstool. She glanced around the small, dimly lit jazz club, wondering whether she'd missed seeing Oliver.

None of the faces lining the distressed brick walls looked familiar. The crowd ranged in ages from early twenties to late sixties. Various nationalities and genders dressed in outfits spanning from sweat suits to cocktail dresses filled the room.

Mona was glad she'd chosen to wear her fitted wool magenta dress and nude patent pumps. The look fell somewhere in the middle of the diverse club goers.

A large group of patrons shuffled through the heavy vintage steel door. They stopped and stared at the black-

and-white photos of famous jazz musicians hanging along the entryway.

Mona stared anxiously at the group, hoping to catch a glimpse of Oliver. But when they shuffled farther inside and stopped at the bar, she realized he wasn't among the crowd.

Please show up, she thought to herself while once again checking his Instagram page.

"I hope I'm at the right place," she muttered aloud. Mona double-checked his latest post.

What's up, my peeps? Who's meeting me at Silvia's Speakeasy tonight? It's open mic night! So come through and check out some of the best musicians in all of Louisiana. Mico will be at the bar serving up his handcrafted holiday cocktails, too. So don't miss out. See you there!

"Okay, I am definitely where I'm supposed to be," Mona said to herself.

She was actually surprised that Oliver was attending yet another social event.

If he shows up, that is...she thought, taking another look around the bar. *Where are you?*

Neither Mona nor Dillon had heard from the Whitmans since visiting their home. She'd tried reaching out to them but got no response. So she had resorted to doing what she did best—stalking Oliver's social media to find out where he'd be.

Now all you need to do is make an appearance.

Mona's cell phone buzzed. A text message from Dillon popped up on the screen.

Hey, Chief Boyer and I had to make an unexpected run to the forensics lab. New DNA results came back on a cold case he'd worked on years ago. He was so pumped that we drove out to Vincent Parish to pick up the report. Heading back that way now. I'll be there as soon as I can. Think you can hang tight until then?

I guess I'll have to, Mona replied. The band will be going on soon. I'll just sip my drink and enjoy the music until you two arrive.

Mona sent the message, then spun around in her stool when she saw a commotion in the back of the bar.

Hands were waving in the air. Shots were being passed around. Patrons were toasting and hugging one another.

Mona stood up to get a better look at the group. As they began to scatter about, Oliver appeared. He was standing off to the side of the crowd, sullenly staring down at the worn hardwood floor.

She quickly grabbed her drink.

Play it cool. Act casually.

Just as she stepped away from the bar, Mona heard a loud voice boom into a microphone.

"Hello everyone, and welcome to Silvia's open mic night!"

Mona turned toward the stage. A heavyset older man with a bald head and triple chin stood front and center. He appeared cool yet jolly in his white button-down shirt, red bow tie, red suspenders and black corduroy pants. He was holding a bottle of beer in one hand and swiping a checkered handkerchief across his forehead with the other.

"I'm your host, Sir LeBlanc. And I'll be keeping you

entertained throughout the evening while introducing some of the best jazz bands in all of Louisiana. So sit back. Relax. Or get up on your feet. Whatever floats your boat. Just make sure you're having a good time and keeping the bartenders busy!"

As Sir LeBlanc announced the first act, Mona turned her attention to the back of the club. Oliver was still standing in the corner. But now, it appeared as though he was in the middle of a heated argument with a petite redhead.

Oh, maybe she's what brought him out tonight...

Mona watched as Oliver placed his hand on the woman's shoulder. She pushed him away, then pointed her finger in his face. After yelling something at him, she stormed into the ladies' room.

Another woman stepped in and grabbed Oliver when he tried to follow her. The two of them got into a shouting match.

"What in the hell is going on?" Mona muttered.

Several moments passed before the woman threw her arms in the air, then ran into the ladies' room.

Oliver spun around and exited the club through the back door.

No! Don't leave!

Mona practically threw her drink down onto the bar. She tucked her gold leather clutch underneath her arm and hurried after him.

"Excuse me!" she yelled at the tight crowd blocking her pathway.

She squeezed her way to the back. By the time she reached the exit, Oliver was long gone.

Mona burst through the door and almost fell down onto the dark alley's black asphalt.

She jumped at the sound of the door slamming behind her.

Calm down, she told herself. *Just find Oliver.*

Her cell phone buzzed. Mona ignored it and turned right, then left. The long alleyway revealed nothing but steamy darkness.

Oliver was nowhere in sight.

The sound of scurrying footsteps echoed off the brick walls lining the alleyway. Mona's ears perked up. It sounded as though the heavy clicking was fading away toward her right.

She set off in the direction of the footsteps echoing against the asphalt.

Mona almost lost her balance when her heels skidded along the damp ground. But she kept going, determined to find Oliver.

She wrinkled her nose after passing a foul-smelling dumpster that reeked of rotten food.

Maybe you should've just stayed inside the club...

A gust of hot steam rushed up from the ground. Mona hopped over a manhole cover, choking on the stifling vapor.

The air cleared. She'd reached the end of the alleyway.

Oliver was still nowhere to be found.

"Dammit," she whispered.

Mona peered down both ends of the unfamiliar street. Aside from a few run-down shacks and small, swampy marshes, the road was deserted.

She parted her lips to call out Oliver's name. But she was interrupted when her cell phone buzzed again.

Mona grabbed it from her clutch. Dillon's name flashed across the screen.

Finally, she thought. *You're here...*

Right before she accepted the call, Mona felt a presence looming over her.

She dropped the phone in her clutch and paused.

Someone was approaching from behind.

Mona spun around.

A masked man grabbed her arm and pulled her in close. He was dressed in all black, just like the shadowy figure out in Beechtree.

Mona screamed, struggling to free herself from his grip.

"What are you *doing*—?"

"Shut up!" the man growled.

Mona clamped her lips together, resisting the urge to scream once again.

Do not show any signs of fear. Do not show any signs of fear...

"What do you want?" she asked, her strong tone contradicting the terror running through her body.

"The better question is, what do *you* want? Why are you still here in Lake Landry, Mona Avery?"

She grimaced when he spoke her name. The thought of being stalked by a maniac chilled her to the bone.

Stand strong. Do not let this man know you're afraid.

"Who are you?" she boldly asked. "And why are you following me?"

"Following you?" he repeated. "Like I did that day you were roaming aimlessly around Beechtree?"

The man's grip on her arm tightened. He moved in closer. Mona cringed when his hot breath blew on her neck.

"To answer your question," he whispered, "I'm following you because I want you to get the *hell* out of Lake Landry!"

Mona winced as an intense pain ripped down her arm. She blinked rapidly, trying to find a familiarity in his voice. She didn't.

His hand slid from her arm down to her waist. Suddenly, Mona was overcome by the urge to fight.

She shoved him as hard as she could, then spun around to run back down the alley.

But before she could move, he threw his arm around her neck, forcing her into a tight choke hold.

"You *bitch*," he barked. "You think you can hurt me? I should kill you just for trying!"

Mona whimpered as the man dragged her toward a dark corner of the alley's entryway. She grabbed his forearm, struggling to loosen his grip. Her heels screeched along the pavement as she fought to stay on her feet.

"Listen to me," the man continued, "and listen to me good. I want you out of this town. *Immediately.* Now, you can do it the easy way and hop on the first flight back to LA. Or you can do it the hard way and simply disappear, just like your girl did…"

Mona gasped at his harsh words. She jerked her head away when his lips brushed against her ear.

"Please," she pleaded, "leave me alone. Let me go!"

"Don't worry, I'll leave you alone. Just as soon as you leave Olivia Whitman's case alone. You're in over your head, Mona Avery. Get out while you can. Consider this your final notice. Got it?"

She remained silent, too stunned to speak.

"No response, huh?" her attacker spewed before pulling a switchblade from his pocket. He waved it in front of her face, then grazed her cheek with the cold, sharp blade.

Stinging tears burned Mona's eyes. She stiffened up, numb with fright.

The man tightened his grip on her neck.

Get to your phone, she thought. *Try to call Dillon back.*

Mona gasped for breath while fumbling for her clutch. She shoved her hand inside and grabbed hold of her phone.

As her trembling fingers struggled to unlock the cell, Mona heard a door open. The sound of voices and footsteps filled the air.

She fought to turn her head and look down the alleyway. *Get noticed. Scream for help.*

Through the corner of her eye, she saw club goers exiting Silvia's and spilling out into the alley. They were laughing and lighting cigarettes.

The attacker loosened his grip on Mona's neck. She inhaled deeply, choking as the air rushed through her lungs.

She once again tore at his arm, struggling to free herself. But he refused to let her go.

"Do the right thing, Mona Avery," he growled. This time, his sinister tone had lowered several octaves. "Get the hell out of Lake Landry. Unless you want your fellow journalists reporting on *your* disappearance."

Just as she felt herself giving up on being freed, the man pushed Mona against a brick wall, then took off running.

She quickly swiped open the camera app on her phone. Mona tried to take a picture of the man. But he had already disappeared into the darkness.

She spun around and stumbled back down the alley. Her hand scaled the wall as she struggled to hold herself up.

"Excuse me, ma'am?" a woman who was standing near Silvia's back door asked her. "Are you all right?"

"I—I'm fine," Mona groaned.

The woman walked over and placed her hand on Mona's arm.

She grimaced, still sore from her attacker's vicious grasp.

"Are you sure you're okay?" the woman probed.

Mona stood straight up and cleared her throat. A small crowd began to gather around her.

Don't make a spectacle of yourself, she thought. *Just get back inside and call Dillon.*

"I'm positive," she managed. "Thank you for asking."

Despite her wobbly legs, Mona was able to make her way back inside of Silvia's. She dialed Dillon's number. The call went straight to voice mail.

"Nooo," she moaned.

At the sound of the beep, she began leaving a message.

"It's Mona," she yelled over the music. "I was—I was just attacked! I'd stepped outside to—"

She stopped abruptly at the sight of Dillon standing near the entrance.

"Dillon!" she screamed.

When he failed to look her way, Mona pushed through the crowd toward the front of the club.

"Hey!" Dillon boomed as she approached him. "Sorry I'm late. You know how long-winded Chief Boyer can be. Did Oliver ever show up?"

Mona just stood there, staring at him.

"Uh-oh," Dillon said. "He's not here, is he? Don't worry. Let's just find a table, have a drink and enjoy the music—"

Before he could finish, Mona collapsed in his arms.

"What—what's going on?" he asked, his heightened tone filled with confusion.

"I was attacked when I went out back to try to find Oliver!" Mona cried into Dillon's chest. "The same man who threatened me in Beechtree followed me here tonight. He pulled a knife on me in the alley behind the club."

"Hold on, hold on," Dillon said, wrapping his arms around her. "Slow down. I can't understand everything you're saying. You were *attacked*?"

Mona looked up at him. "Yes. Can we please get out of here?"

"Wait! Do you think he's still in the area? I can call backup and search the perimeter and—"

"Dillon, no. He's long gone. Trust me, you won't find him. Now, please, I have got to get out of here."

"Of course. Come on."

Dillon held her tightly while leading her out of the club.

"Did you drive yourself here?" he asked.

"No. I took an Uber."

"Okay. Let's get you back to the inn."

They took the short walk down the block to his car in silence. Once they climbed inside and Dillon pulled off, Mona was overcome by a wave of emotion. She leaned her head against the back of the seat and closed her eyes, stunned that she'd been assaulted.

"I cannot believe this happened to me," she whispered.

"I can't either. And I'm so sorry. Can you tell me exactly what happened?"

Mona opened her eyes and took a deep breath. "I was sitting at the bar inside of Silvia's when I spotted Oliver. After getting into an altercation with a couple of women, he ran out of the club's back door. So I went after him."

She paused, her voice shaking with fear.

Dillon reached over and took her hand in his. Her fingers tightened around his palm. His reassuring touch gave her the strength to continue.

"When I ran out into the alleyway, Oliver was nowhere in sight. So I made a right turn and followed what I thought was the sound of his footsteps. And then, out of nowhere, I was attacked by the same man who followed me out to Beechtree."

"How do you know it was the same man? Did you get a good look at him?"

"No. He was wearing a ski mask. But I recognized the outfit and build. Not to mention he told me that it was him. Thank God I'm okay. He did, however, rough me up and pull a knife on me. And he said that if I don't stop investigating Olivia's disappearance and leave town, I'm going to go missing, too."

Mona felt Dillon's grasp on her hand tighten. She looked over at him.

His expression was tense.

He suddenly slammed on the brakes and turned the car around.

"What are you doing?" she asked.

"Going back to Silvia's. I've gotta track this maniac down."

"Dillon, I'm sure he's long gone by now."

His lips twisted in disappointment. "You're probably right." He slowly turned the car back around and headed in the opposite direction.

"I'm so sorry this happened," Mona told him.

"No, *I'm* sorry this happened," he insisted, pressing down on the accelerator.

She turned and looked out the window, watching as they sped past The Bayou Inn and made a sharp left turn down Robinson Avenue.

"Where are you going?" she asked.

"To the police station. I know you may not feel up to it, but after tonight's assault, I want to file a report ASAP. Do you think you can do that?"

Mona's heart began to race at the thought of going to the station and repeating the details of the attack. But she knew it was necessary.

"Yes," she told Dillon. "I can do that. And afterward, I think we need to come up with a new game plan."

"Okay. Do you already have a strategy in mind?"

Mona looked down and pressed her shaky hands together. "I do. For starters, while I fully believe Blake is behind all this, I don't think he's the one who attacked me."

"You don't? Are you sure?"

"I'm positive. The assailant's voice and physical stature are the complete opposite of Blake's. But I wouldn't put it past him to send one of his guys after me. So, with that being said, I want to approach Blake again and request an on-air interview. This time, I'll present it as if I want to help him prove his innocence to the people of Lake Landry."

"*What? But...why?*"

"Because I really want to get him in front of the camera. And when I do, the entire country will witness me eat him alive. By the time I'm done, he will have admitted to the crimes he committed against Olivia *and* me without even knowing it."

"Whoa," Dillon said, cracking a smile as he pulled in front of the station. "Somebody got their chutzpah back."

"It never left. It was just buried underneath a layer of terror. And that's quickly fading, by the way. Now I'm bound and determined to prove Blake's guilt."

"Okay, well, if you can pull the confession out of him that law enforcement couldn't, which we all know Mona Avery is perfectly capable of doing, then I say go for it."

"Thank you. I will. Oh, and even though tonight was a total bust, I still haven't given up on scoring interviews with the Whitmans. Especially Oliver."

"Good. You shouldn't give up."

Dillon reached for his door handle, then paused.

"Listen," he continued. "Before we go inside, let me assure you I'm going to do all that I can to protect you from here on out. If that means escorting you everywhere you go, and having a patrol car keep watch over The Bayou Inn, then so be it. And if you land that interview with Blake, I will be tagging along. Also, no more roaming around in desolate areas or down dark alleyways."

"But this time, I was—"

"Hold on," he interrupted. "Let me finish. I'm not blaming you for what happened tonight. I'm just saying that we need to take extra precautions to help keep you safe now that we know you're being followed. My partner back in Baton Rouge had a habit of going out on his own to investigate cases. One night when he was by himself, he ended up getting severely injured. That was another reason why I left town. It got to be too much. I don't want to end up in a situation like that with you."

"Understood," Mona replied quietly. "And thank you."

"You're welcome. But I like where your head's at regarding Blake and the interview. I think it's a good idea. You've got my full support."

"Thanks, Dillon. That means a lot to me."

"Of course. Now, let's go inside and get this report filed. Then we'll go back to the inn, have a drink and decompress."

Mona took a deep breath and opened her car door.

"You good?" Dillon asked her. "Are you sure you're up for this, or would you rather wait until tomorrow?"

She could still feel her limbs trembling from the aftermath of the attack.

Pull it together, she told herself. *You can do this. Nobody said your job would be easy. You were built for this.*

"Yes," she said, holding her head high as if that would pump confidence into her veins. "I'm good. Let's do this."

Dillon gave her arm a reassuring squeeze. Together, they walked inside the police station.

Chapter Ten

Dillon sat in the corner of Blake's study, staring up at the elaborate dome-shaped ceiling. Soft yellow recessed lights shone down on rich, sandalwood walls. The curved shelves were packed with antique books, family photos and expensive heirlooms. Tufted cream leather furniture surrounded an intricately carved, custom-built desk.

He took a sip of ice water. He glanced over at Mona, whose makeup artist was busy dusting bronzer across her cheekbones. A cameraman adjusted the light hanging above her chair as she straightened the sleeves on her lavender cape-back dress.

Blake walked over and took a seat across from Mona. As soon as he settled in, a producer approached him and attached a lavalier microphone to his navy blue blazer's lapel. He appeared calm and collected while sipping coffee from a marble ceramic mug.

Dillon shifted in his chair. He adjusted his tan suede sports jacket, then smoothed his dark denim jeans.

Between Blake's designer suit and Mona's elaborate getup, he felt severely underdressed. But he quickly reminded himself that he wouldn't be the one in front of the camera. He'd simply tagged along to support

Mona and make sure things went smoothly during the interview.

Just as she'd planned, Mona was able to convince Blake that going live on air and openly discussing Olivia's disappearance would help salvage his reputation. His attorneys, who were sitting across the room quietly eyeing their cell phones, thought otherwise. But there was nothing they could say to convince the narcissistic Blake Carter that doing a live broadcast with Mona was a bad idea.

Dillon was still shocked that he'd agreed to it. But at the same time, he wasn't. Blake believed he could outsmart anyone. That included Mona, law enforcement, the community, and anyone else who dared to go up against him.

"But this is Mona Avery we're talking about," Dillon had overheard one of Blake's attorneys telling him when they first arrived at the house. "The woman is a pro. She can catch you up and have you twisting your words, then confessing to things you had nothing to do with."

"Not me," Blake replied before popping his crisp white collar. "Around here? *I'm* the pro. Now step aside and watch me work, gentlemen."

And that was it. Blake's attorneys backed off and took a seat in the corner. Considering how much they were probably getting paid, Dillon wasn't shocked that they'd given up so easily.

"How are we looking on time?" Mona asked her producer. "Are we just about ready to go live?"

"We are," she replied, stepping back while the makeup artist swooped in and brushed a curl away from Mona's face.

Dillon watched as Mona stared at Blake. He could see the glint in her shining eyes. He knew she was probably thinking of the attacks she'd endured.

May God have mercy on your soul, he thought, knowing that Mona would live up to her words and eat Blake alive.

"Okay, everyone," the producer said, "going live in five, four, three, two…"

She pointed at Mona, who turned and looked directly into the camera.

"Hello, everyone. Thank you for joining me during this special broadcast. Today I am here with Blake Carter, a well-known businessman who lives in Lake Landry, Louisiana. As many of you know, I've been in Lake Landry for the past few weeks investigating the disappearance of my good friend Olivia Whitman. Blake is the husband of Olivia, and many believe that he is involved in her disappearance."

Oh! Dillon thought. *So you're just gonna come out swinging. Okay…*

He turned to Blake, expecting to see some sort of reaction. But he just sat there, his expression appearing steadfast and unruffled.

"Blake has agreed to sit down with me to discuss Olivia's case," Mona continued, "in hopes of clearing his name and leading investigators to the real perpetrators. Blake, thank you for joining me."

"Thank you for having me," he replied coolly.

"So, I'm just going to go ahead and ask the question that everyone wants to know. Did you have anything to do with Olivia's disappearance?"

Blake's eyebrows shot up into his forehead.

"No, I did not," he responded, his quiet tone tinged with pain. "And I resent you even asking me that."

"Do you have any idea what may have happened to her?"

"No, I do not. But I hope that she will return home soon, safe and sound."

"*Humph*, do you now..." Mona replied, her wide eyes filled with skepticism. "Let's go back to the day that Olivia went missing. What was her mood? Did she seem worried? Or had she mentioned anything about feeling unsafe?"

Blake turned his head slightly, staring at Mona through the corner of his eye. Dillon was baffled by his silence. But then he remembered Mona telling him that Blake hadn't seen Olivia the day she went missing because he'd spent the night at his mistress's house.

"Oh wait," Mona said. "That's right. You told me during an earlier conversation that you didn't see Olivia the day she went missing. You weren't home that morning."

"No. I wasn't. I was away on business."

Mona threw Blake a doubtful look before continuing. "All right, then. So anyway, how long was Olivia missing before her disappearance was reported to police?"

Blake paused. Dillon could see his jaws clenching from across the room. It was clear that Mona was getting under his skin.

You've been fooled, man, he thought to himself amusingly. *Mona came here to take you down, and she's doing just that...*

"About a week, I believe?" Blake said, crossing one leg over the other.

"A whole week? *Wow.* That's a pretty long time, isn't it? Why'd you wait so long?"

Mona glared at Blake so fiercely that Dillon felt an outbreak of sweat form along his own hairline.

"Oh wait," Mona continued without allowing him to respond. "You can't answer that, can you? Because you weren't the one who reported Olivia missing. Her mother was. Why is that, Blake? Why didn't *you* inform police that your wife was missing? If you had, maybe she would've been found by now. I'm sure you know that the first forty-eight hours into an investigation are the most important, don't you?"

"I'm sorry," one of Blake's attorneys interrupted as he stood up. "But we're going to have to stop this—"

"No, no," Blake said, holding his hand in the air without taking his eyes off Mona. "It's fine. We can continue."

The attorney shook his head from side to side before slowly sitting back down.

"As you know, Mona," Blake said, "my marriage to Olivia wasn't in the best place. We got together when we were fairly young. The stress of our jobs, the pressure of upholding our prestigious families' names, our desire to start a family—"

"*Your* desire to start a family," Mona interjected. "From what I understand, Olivia did not want to have children with you. As a matter of fact, she was preparing to file for divor—"

"I'm sorry," Blake smirked, interrupting Mona's scathing rant. "But were you a part of my marriage, Mona? How would you know the intimate details of our relationship? Idle gossip doesn't compare to conversations between a husband and wife. However, you probably wouldn't understand that. Because you don't have a husband, do you?"

Dillon felt his breath catch in his throat. He peered over at Mona.

"No. I don't," she replied, staring icily at him.

"Exactly," Blake continued condescendingly. "So see, if you're ever blessed enough to actually find a husband, you'll realize that things occur within a marriage that aren't shared with outsiders. My wife and I love one another, Mona. And while we may have been having a few issues, we were in fact discussing starting a family."

"So then why wouldn't you have immediately reported your beloved wife missing, Blake?"

"Because I just assumed she'd gone off to clear her head. You know, take some time to be alone. But here's my question to you, Mona. As her friend, how come *you* didn't realize Olivia was missing? Since you seem to know so much about my marriage and what she was going through, you should've known she'd disappeared. Then *you* could've been the one to contact the police."

"This isn't about me, Blake. And I am not a suspect."

"Last time I checked, neither am I. Am I right, Detective Reed?" he asked, pointing over at Dillon.

Dillon wished he could've fallen through the floor as the camera turned toward him.

"No," he replied quietly. "You're not."

"I didn't think so," Blake gloated before turning back to Mona. "Maybe you need to reevaluate your friendship with my wife. Sounds like you two aren't as close as you may have thought. Next question."

Dillon looked over at Mona. The anger underneath

her steely glare was apparent. She sat up in her chair, her back rigid.

He wanted to go over and embrace her reassuringly. Let her know she was doing a good job. But he couldn't. So he remained seated, hoping she could feel his support from the sidelines.

"Blake, what have you done to help find your wife?" she asked.

Nice comeback, he thought. *Stay on track. Don't let this man rattle you...*

"I've actually done a lot," he boasted. "Leo Mendez, who is Transformation Cosmetics' director of operations, has done a tremendous job in helping to plan a couple of search party efforts. He even assisted Olivia's family in planning a vigil shortly after she went missing."

Mona cocked her head to the side. "Wait, this Leo Mendez, he did all of that work on your behalf?"

"Yes, he did. At my request, of course."

"Wasn't he also Oliver Whitman's boss when he worked at Transformation Cosmetics?"

"That is correct. And per usual, Leo stepped up to the plate and showed immense leadership when he terminated Oliver."

Dillon leaned forward, intrigued by Blake's version of his encounter with Oliver. He hoped Mona would allow him to delve a little further.

When Mona propped her hand underneath her chin and stared at Blake curiously, he knew she was just as intrigued as he was.

"I don't want to get too off track with this interview," she stated, "but do you think Oliver has a good relationship with his sister?"

Blake sat back in his chair and crossed his arms. "Not at all. His parents had threatened to cut him off financially. He still depends on Mommy and Daddy, and they're sick of it. So he was growing more and more resentful by the day. His jealousy toward Olivia's success was eating away at him, too. It's no secret she's the Whitmans' golden child and he's the black sheep. As a matter of fact, you probably need to be questioning *his* involvement in her disappearance—"

"Hold on," Mona interrupted. "Let's reel it in. I don't want to discuss Oliver's possible involvement. He's not here to defend himself. So why don't we get back to you and the missing person events Leo coordinated. Did you assist him in *any* of the planning?"

Blake shifted in his seat, glancing over at his attorneys. After several seconds of silence, he turned back to Mona.

"No. I didn't."

"Did you attend any of the events?"

"I, um…no. I had a couple of unexpected work emergencies pop up." Blake paused. He raised his head and stared down his nose at Mona. "But wait, did *you* attend any of the events?"

"I hadn't arrived in town yet," she quickly shot back. "However, now that I'm here, I am doing all that I can to help find Olivia."

"Good. So am I."

"Really? How so?" Mona probed, tapping her alligator leather fountain pen against her cheek.

"For starters, I've cooperated with law enforcement one hundred percent throughout this entire investigation. When they asked to come and search our house, I let them. When they asked to search our vehicles, I let them. When they confiscated our computers, I let them. When I was asked to turn over my cell phone, I did. When they asked for a DNA sample, I gave it to them. There is nothing I haven't done to assist in the effort to find my wife."

Mona's eyes squinted. She stared daggers at Blake while pursing her lips.

Dillon watched her closely, rubbing his hands together while anxiously awaiting the next question.

"And that polygraph test you took," she continued.

"Yes, what about it?"

"You didn't pass it."

"The test came back *no opinion*."

"Meaning?"

Blake sighed heavily. His eyes diverted to the floor as they quickly filled with tears. "Mona, I got so emotional while trying to answer the questions that the examiner kept having to stop and restart the test. As a result of that, he couldn't get an exact reading."

"So again, you didn't pass the test," she said, appearing unmoved by his show of emotion.

"The point is, I didn't fail the test."

"Yet the entire town of Lake Landry believes you had something to do with Olivia's disappearance."

Blake ran his hand across his face and opened his mouth to object. But Mona kept going before he could get a word out.

"What about Olivia's life insurance policy? Can we talk about that?"

"Sure," he sniffed. "What about it?"

"You increased the amount of your wife's payout. A *week* before she went missing."

"Yes. *We* did."

"But you didn't increase yours. Why is that?"

Blake emitted a condescending chuckle.

"Mona, here's something else you may not understand as a single woman with…no children, isn't that correct?" he asked, tilting his head while scratching his scalp.

"Oh boy," Dillon whispered, hoping Mona wouldn't implode live on air. He noticed Blake's attorneys over in the corner, smirking and nodding their heads at one another.

Idiots, he thought before turning his attention back to the interview.

"Once again, Blake, this isn't about me. This is about you and your missing wife. Now please. Answer the question."

"Well, as a husband who's planning a family with my wife, Olivia and I wanted to increase the amounts on our life insurance policies for the benefit of our future children."

"But that still doesn't explain why Olivia's policy was increased and yours wasn't."

"Olivia was able to contact our insurance agent and adjust her policy before I did." He shrugged nonchalantly. "It's as simple as that. You do know that I am the president of Transformation Cosmetics. So, I'm a pretty busy man. But trust me, I was planning on increasing my payout, as well."

The room fell silent. Mona shuffled the papers sitting in her lap. Dillon could see her hands trembled from where he was sitting.

Uh-oh, he thought. *Come on, Mona. Hang in there. Don't lose your cool.*

"You okay over there?" Blake asked her, the snark in his tone apparent.

"I'm fine," Mona said. "Just looking for my next question."

Blake leaned forward, sneering at her.

"Wow," he breathed. "Mona Avery, getting thrown off her game by little ole me. What is the world coming to?"

When Blake turned to the camera and smiled, Mona tossed her papers down onto the floor.

"What about Olivia's bloodstained necklace, Blake?" she spat. "Why don't you explain *that* to me and my viewers?"

"Excuse me?" Blake asked, gripping the arms of his chair. "What are you talking about? What bloodstained necklace?"

Dillon jumped up. The producer ran over and grabbed him before he could interrupt the interview.

"The necklace that I found in Beechtree near the water source where Olivia went missing," Mona continued. "Her blood and *your* DNA were found on it. Now, how can you explain that?"

"I have no idea what the hell you're talking about!" Blake yelled, standing up and ripping off his mic. "Frank," he said to his attorney, "what is going on here?"

"I don't have a clue," he replied, approaching the pair.

"Don't stop rolling tape," Dillon heard the producer say to the cameraman.

"That's enough," Dillon said, brushing past the producer and stepping in between Mona and Blake. "This interview is over. Steve, could you please cut the camera?"

"Detective Reed," Frank said, "I think you've got some explaining to do. Is there any truth to Ms. Avery's claim?"

"I'm sorry, but at this time, I am not at liberty to discuss the details surrounding the investigation. If I need to bring your client in again for questioning, I will do so."

Blake snickered sarcastically while buttoning his suit jacket. "So what you're saying is, after Mona's little outburst, you still don't have any viable evidence linking me to Olivia's disappearance. And while I have not formally been named a suspect, I'm not even a person of interest. Is that correct?"

Dillon turned to him, fighting the urge to knock the arrogant grin off his face. "Mr. Carter, if there is any information that needs to be shared with you, I'll do so. In the meantime, we're done here. Mona, let's go."

His chest heaved as he watched Mona pack up her things. He couldn't believe she'd lost her cool and revealed intricate details of their investigation, not only to Blake and his attorneys, but to all of her viewers.

When Blake's lawyers pulled him to the side, the cameraman turned to the producer. "Should I stop filming now?"

Dillon threw his arms out at his sides. "You're still taping all of this?"

"Yes," Steve replied sheepishly, his eyes darting back and forth between Dillon and the producer.

Dillon turned back to Mona. Every nerve in his body was burning with anger.

"Could you please hurry up? I need to get out of this house. *Now*."

"I'm coming," she snapped.

As Mona continued gathering her things, the producer approached her.

"I know this interview didn't go as you'd planned, but it is ratings *gold*. Viewers are flooding our social media sites with questions and comments about Olivia's disappearance."

"Yeah, well, hopefully in the midst of all the chatter, we'll get some solid tips that'll lead to Blake's arrest."

Dillon shook his head in disgust.

"What it'll likely lead to is the media circus and public frenzy that I've been wanting to avoid this entire time," he interjected. "Now can we please get the hell out of here?"

Mona ignored him and turned her attention to her producer. "Sarah, would you mind wrapping up this segment for me? Maybe cut back to the reporters who are on standby back at the studio in LA? They can announce that due to unforeseen circumstances, Blake's interview had to be cut short, then move on to another story that I had on the docket."

"Of course," Sarah replied without looking up at Mona. Her head was buried in her phone. "Wow, the social media team has already uploaded a clip of the interview to Instagram. The post has over two thousand comments! This is wild…"

Steve peered over Sarah's shoulder and stared at her phone.

"Ooh, that is so cool! Did they give me filming credit?"

Dillon balled his hands into tight fists and turned to Mona.

"Will you please—"

"I'm ready," she quickly told him. "Let's go."

He stormed through the study, turning toward Blake on the way out.

"I'll be in touch," he barked.

"Yeah, and so will my attorneys!" Blake shot back.

Dillon practically ran through the foyer. His vision was so blurred with rage that he almost crashed into the eight-foot-tall Christmas tree standing in front of a massive bay window.

Crystal bells hanging from its branches jingled when his arm brushed up against them. But he wasn't concerned about damaging any ornaments. He was too focused on escaping the Carter residence.

Dillon swung open the wooden double front doors and hurried down the veranda's stairs two at a time.

"Dillon," Mona breathed as the pair walked along the winding driveway.

He ignored her, rushing toward the car and opening the passenger door without saying a word.

Mona paused before slipping inside. She stood in front of him, as if waiting to make eye contact. But he focused on the lush wooded area across from the house, unable to look her in the eyes.

"Look," she began. "I am really sorry about what happened in there. I don't know what came over me. You know I am a consummate professional. I *never* crack like that. Maybe I lost it because this case is so personal to me. Please know that I did not mean to bring up the necklace. But Blake just kept poking and poking and—"

"This isn't Blake's fault, Mona," Dillon interrupted. "So you can't blame him. And I *thought* you were a consummate professional, which is why I agreed to partner with you on this investigation. But once again, here I am. Having second thoughts."

"Dillon, please. Don't start second-guessing me. Today was a mistake. I'm human. I allowed my emotions to get the best of me. But trust me. It won't happen again."

"Oh, I know it won't. Because I'm going to talk to Chief Boyer about taking you off of this case. I think it's time for you to go home to Colorado and spend the holidays with your family. Let law enforcement take over from here. Not only have you become a loose cannon, but the investigation is getting too dangerous for you to remain on board anyway."

Mona stood there, her mouth falling open. But nothing came out. She just stared at him through squinting eyes.

Dillon felt bits of sympathy trying to seep through his wall of anger. But he was too upset to empathize with her.

"We should get going," he said, his cold, hardened demeanor reminding him of the days when he worked in Baton Rouge. "I need to get down to the station and do some damage control. Call a meeting with the officers to plan out a new strategy on how we're going to tackle Olivia's disappearance moving forward."

"Fine," Mona muttered. She climbed inside the car and slammed the door.

"I can't believe this…" Dillon said to himself as he walked around to the driver's side.

He hated the volatile way in which he and Mona's partnership had ended. But he could no longer afford to keep her on the biggest case of his career.

Chapter Eleven

Mona jumped at the sound of her pinging cell phone. She grabbed it, hoping Dillon's name would flash across the screen.

"Ugh," she sighed after seeing it was yet another text message from her boss.

She slid the phone across the black wrought iron table without opening the message.

She was sitting on the inn's quaint back patio, taking a much-needed break over a glass of spiced iced tea and a plate of charbroiled oysters.

It had been several days since she'd last spoken to Dillon. Mona had reached out to him numerous times, but he refused to return her calls and texts.

Mona's viewers, however, couldn't get enough of her. After the interview with Blake aired, her cell phone, email inbox and social media platforms had been blowing up.

But the increase in popularity had done nothing to assist authorities in Olivia's disappearance. It actually appeared to hinder it.

The public began treating the case as salacious tabloid fodder rather than a serious missing person investigation. Mona feared that potential witnesses were turned off by the spectacle that the case had become, and decided to keep pertinent information to themselves in order to avoid the circus.

Exactly what Dillon feared the most. All thanks to me...

Mona's cell phone rang. Her heart bounced into her throat at the thought of it being Dillon. She groaned loudly after seeing it was her boss, who'd resorted to calling instead of texting.

"Hey, Felix," she said after picking up the call. "What's going on?"

"*You're* what's going on, my dear," he boomed so loudly that she had to pull the phone away from her ear. "Who knew that my star investigative journalist could somehow manage to shine even brighter? You knocked it out of the park with that Blake Carter interview!"

"Yeah. So says the viewers, but...I'm kind of seeing things differently on my end."

"You are? How? Why?"

"I allowed Blake to break me, Felix. I lost my cool live on air. I am mortified by how I let that man get the best of me."

"Are you kidding? Mona, you broke exclusive news to our viewers that no one knew about. Not even Olivia's own family! Do you know how much credibility that has given CNB News?"

"Sure, but do you know how many times Olivia's parents have called me asking why news of the necklace wasn't shared with them first? And of course they're thinking that Olivia was murdered since I revealed that her blood was found on it. Mr. and Mrs. Whitman are absolutely hysterical, and it's all my fault."

"The truth hurts, Mona. I'm sorry Olivia's parents

had to face that news, but you were just reporting the facts of the case. That's part of your job."

"Felix, you're missing the point. I have personal relationships with these people. And now, thanks to my on-air explosion, the Whitmans are demanding that authorities arrest Blake immediately. Of course they can't because there isn't enough evidence against him. So now they're getting their attorneys involved. I'm telling you, my interview has turned this case into an absolute mess."

"Sounds to me like you're worried about things that you shouldn't be concerned with. Come on, superstar. Your ratings are through the roof. Let's focus on that and let Lake Landry's police department handle the rest."

Mona threw her head back in exasperation. "You just don't get it," she muttered more to herself than her boss.

She stared up at the pale green petals hanging from the American fringe trees lining the patio's white wooden fence.

Where do I go from here? she asked herself.

"So, speaking of the Whitmans," Felix continued, "I've been reading the comments on CNB's website. Viewers really want to see you sit down with that brother of Olivia's. Do you think you can land an interview with him?"

"After what happened during Blake's interview? I highly doubt it. I was actually going to try to schedule an interview with Oliver the night that I was attacked."

"Yeah," Felix replied quietly. "I'm so sorry that happened to you. Have the authorities made any progress on an arrest? Or even identified a suspect?"

"Not yet, unfortunately. But I'm hoping that—"

Mona was interrupted when Evelyn walked out onto the patio.

"Hold on a sec, Felix."

"How's it going out here?" Evelyn asked her.

"Fine, thanks. Everything is delicious."

"Good, glad to hear it. Listen, there's a woman named Bonnie here asking for you. She said she's a friend of a friend. She was acting pretty peculiar, so I told her to wait in the lobby while I came back to ask if you know her."

Mona's eyes squinted as she stared at Evelyn blankly. "Bonnie, Bonnie... Oh! Yes, I know who she is. That's Olivia's coworker. She's here to see me?"

"Yes. Is it okay if I bring her back?"

"Please, thank you."

"No problem. Be right back."

After Evelyn walked off, Mona turned her attention back to her phone call.

"Felix, it looks like I may have a new lead. That co-worker of Olivia's who I met with a couple of weeks ago is here to see me."

"Really? You think she's got more info to share?"

"I hope so. I highly doubt she would've just shown up at the inn unannounced unless she did. But we'll see."

Mona looked up and saw Bonnie following Evelyn out onto the patio. She was clutching her purse strap tightly. Her complexion appeared pale while her fallen expression was wrought with worry.

"Listen, Bonnie's on her way over. I'll call you back as soon as we're done."

"Please do. Talk soon."

Mona disconnected the call and stood up.

"Bonnie, hi. Nice to see you again."

"Yes, same here," she replied hesitantly before turning toward Evelyn. "Would you mind bringing me a glass of ice water?"

"Of course not. Would you like to see a lunch menu, as well?"

"Oh no. Food is the last thing on my mind. Just the water, please. Thank you."

"Coming right up."

As soon as Evelyn was out of earshot, Mona placed her hand gently on Bonnie's shoulder.

"Are you okay?" she asked.

"Yes. Not really. Actually…no. Mind if I sit?"

"Please do. What's going on?"

Bonnie practically crumpled into the chair across from Mona's.

"I've got some new information that may have something to do with Olivia's disappearance."

"Really?"

Mona's heart began to beat faster at the sound of those words. She slowly took a seat, her eyes glued to Bonnie. "What have you heard?"

"It's not what I've heard. It's what I read."

"What you *read*? What do you mean?"

Bonnie paused when Evelyn approached the table with her water.

"Thank you," she mumbled before grabbing the glass and taking several long sips.

"No problem. If you need anything else, just give me a holler."

"Will do."

Once Evelyn was gone, Bonnie continued.

"My supervisor handed over several of Olivia's files

to me that she'd been working on before her disappearance. He asked if I'd review them to make sure the research had been completed."

Bonnie paused, reaching inside her purse and grabbing a tissue.

When she dabbed the corners of her damp eyes, Mona slid to the edge of her chair.

"So what happened?" Mona asked. "Did you see something in one of the files that upset you?"

"Yes," Bonnie sniffed. "One of the companies Olivia was investigating was Alnico Aluminum Corporation. They're notorious for dumping harmful chemicals into residential water sources. I'm talking lead and chromium. Waste that could kill someone if it were to be consumed."

Mona slowly leaned back in her chair, her mind churning in several different directions. She watched as Bonnie reached in her purse again and pulled out a piece of paper.

"Olivia had recently received a third round of test results back from the lab," she continued. "Like the first two, there was proof that residential water sources located near Alnico Aluminum had been contaminated. They contained extraordinarily high levels of carcinogens. Coincidentally, Olivia was preparing to report her findings to the government right before she went missing."

"Oh wow," Mona breathed, her lungs feeling as though they were beginning to constrict. She crossed her arms in front of her and stared up at the sky. "Do you think someone at Alnico found out about Olivia's report and did something to silence her before it could be submitted?"

"Absolutely."

Bonnie unfolded the piece of paper she'd been clutching and slid it across the table.

"Olivia had printed out this email message and added it to the file. It was sent to her by an Alnico executive named George Williamson."

Mona leaned forward and quickly scanned the message.

"As you can see," Bonnie continued, "George told Olivia that he'd received disturbing news from an inside source at LLL Water Quality Laboratory. He doesn't say exactly what it was, but I'm assuming one of our coworkers leaked the information that was in Olivia's report to this George person."

"And I see here that he asked Olivia to meet with him so they could discuss Alnico's waste disposal process in person."

"Yes, which would be unethical according to LLL's company policy. You'd be surprised by the amount of bribery that goes on in this business. These corporations will do anything to avoid being reported to the government. But the act of illegally dumping waste is a common occurrence among these corporations. Doing it the right way, through a certified disposal service, can be costly."

"You'd think that wouldn't be a problem considering how much money these companies make."

"You would think," Bonnie agreed. "But some of them are greedy enough to cut costs by any means necessary. Even if it means poisoning residential water sources."

"That's a damn shame," Mona scoffed. "Not only is it corrupt, but it's just inhumane."

"Yes, it is. And Olivia wasn't having it. Flip the page over and you'll see her response to George's message. She politely turned down his request to meet."

Mona turned the page and skimmed the reply. "This is good. I'm glad Olivia thought enough to keep a paper trail of her interactions with the company, too."

"Oh, Olivia was the queen of maintaining paper trails. In this business, it's imperative that we keep track of all communication between the lab and our clients so as not to misconstrue our findings and their responses."

"Smart. Hey, is it okay if I keep this email?"

"Of course," Bonnie told her. "I made that copy for you. I kept the original in the file."

"Good thinking. Thanks."

Mona's first instinct was to call up her CNB producer and cameraman, rush into Alnico's offices and pay George a visit. Catching him off guard on camera would be priceless. That type of exclusive, investigative reporting is what viewers expected of her. More important, questioning him could lead to Olivia's whereabouts.

But then, Mona paused. She thought about Dillon. She'd already messed up by revealing confidential details about the necklace live on air.

Despite being tempted to put her journalistic skills to work, Mona knew the right thing to do would be to take this information straight to law enforcement.

"So," Bonnie said, snapping Mona out of her thoughts, "has this new development changed your views on Blake's involvement in Olivia's disappearance?"

"Hmm…" Mona sighed, propping her elbows onto her chair's wrought iron arms. "Possibly. But I don't know if I'm ready to let Blake off the hook just yet. What about you? Knowing all that you do about their relationship, has it changed yours?"

Bonnie threw her head back and closed her eyes. "I'm torn, too," she moaned. "After seeing your interview with him, I still sensed a layer of guilt hidden underneath his smug demeanor. But I know more about his lifestyle than the average viewer, so I may be biased."

"Right. But what if the guilt you sensed was attributed to his infidelity? Just because the man is a philanderer doesn't necessarily mean he's a criminal, too."

"That's true. Overall, the interview was pretty explosive. I didn't know Olivia's necklace had been found near the water source she'd been researching. Did that provide law enforcement with any solid leads?"

"No," Mona replied quietly. "Not yet."

"So this necklace that was found. Did the DNA results—"

"I'm sorry, Bonnie. I'm not able to discuss the details of the investigation. I shouldn't have revealed what I did live on air like that. But that damn Blake had pissed me off so badly. I just… I lost control."

"Well, who could blame you! He's such a jerk. I have to admit, though, after hearing that Olivia's necklace was found in Beechtree, then seeing this email from Alnico, I am having second thoughts about Blake's involvement."

"Really? Why?" Mona asked before taking a sip of her tea.

Bonnie paused, staring across the table at Mona with her head tilted curiously.

"Because Alnico is located right outside of Beech-tree."

"Wait, *what*?" Mona choked. "Alnico is located where?"

"Right outside of Beechtree. I'm sorry. I thought you knew that. The water source Olivia was researching is where Alnico had been dumping waste. That connection is why I copied this email and booked it straight over here to see you."

"And I'm so glad you did," Mona said before standing up and shoving the paper inside her tote bag. "Listen, I need to go. I've got to get down to the police station and share this information. It may very well take this investigation in a completely different direction. Bonnie, I can't thank you enough for sharing it with me."

"Of course," Bonnie replied, standing up and following Mona to the front of the inn. "I hope it helps. I just really wanna get to the bottom of all this. Olivia's disappearance has the entire town of Lake Landry shaken up. She was such a big part of this community. And she is sorely missed."

"I know she is. And I'm going to continue doing all that I can to help bring her back. Thank you again for this info."

"You're welcome. Just be careful with it."

"I will."

Mona waved at Bonnie and hopped inside her car, anxious to get to the station and share the new developments with Chief Boyer.

Maybe this'll get me back in Dillon's good graces, she couldn't help but think.

Chapter Twelve

"I know she messed up," Chief Boyer said to Dillon. "But I've known Mona for years. I can assure you that this was just a one-time slipup that'll never happen again."

"Chief, I hear you. But with all due respect, I just can't take that chance again. After she went out to Beechtree behind my back and could have gotten herself killed, she promised there would be no more mistakes. Then what does she do? Go live on air and reveal confidential details about the case that I did not want to get out. Now I've got the Whitmans calling me every single day, demanding answers and threatening to sue me. And have you looked outside?"

Chief Boyer leaned against Dillon's metal-framed doorway and crossed his arms over his protruding belly.

"Yes. I have. And a couple of officers are out there manning the parking lot, asking that the news media pack up and leave. But you know how those reporters are. They're like wild, rabid animals pursuing their prey. You do know they're waiting for you to come out and give a statement, don't you?"

"I do. I've had to utilize the good ole 'I have nothing to report at this time' several times today. And it's going to stay that way until I solve this case."

"Yeah, well, I still believe that Mona is one of your biggest allies. And let's be honest. She didn't do any real harm with that Blake Carter interview. Chalk it up to her being human. And upset that her friend is missing. And remember, you wouldn't have that necklace in evidence if it weren't for her. So don't count Mona out just yet."

"Yes," Dillon heard a woman's voice chirp. "Don't count me out just yet."

Chief Boyer stepped to the side, and Mona appeared in Dillon's doorway.

"I—um…*hey*," he stammered, caught completely off guard. "I wasn't expecting to see you here."

"I wasn't expecting to be here. Yet, here I am…"

"Well, Mona," Chief Boyer interjected after an awkward silence, "just know that you're always welcome. It's good to see you."

"Good to see you, too, Chief. I noticed there's a ton of news media swarming the station."

"Comes with the territory when you're investigating a high-profile case."

"That it does," Mona agreed.

Dillon watched from behind his desk as the pair bantered back and forth.

He couldn't seem to stop his eyes from penetrating Mona's sexy silhouette. Soft curls cascaded beautifully along the sides of her face. The gloss on her supple lips shimmered as she spoke to the chief. Her body swayed like a dancer when she shifted her weight from right to left, showcasing her curvy hips.

Mona's fitted peach turtleneck outlined her figure

in a way that caused a rousing sensation to stir deep within Dillon. He shifted in his chair when she slid her perfectly manicured hands inside the pockets of her snug chocolate brown riding pants.

Get ahold of yourself...

Dillon loosened his gray wool houndstooth tie as waves of heat crept up his neck.

"Listen," Chief Boyer said to Mona, "I'm glad you stopped by. I'm sure you and Detective Reed have a lot to catch up on. So I'll leave you both to it."

He gradually stepped away from the door, glancing over at Dillon and nodding his head.

Dillon stood up and adjusted his pants.

"Thanks, Chief. I've got it from here."

After Chief Boyer closed the door behind him, Mona remained near the doorway, wringing her hands.

"Please," Dillon said, sensing her nervousness, "have a seat."

"Thanks."

Mona walked tentatively toward the desk and waited for him to sit down before following suit.

Dillon felt a pull of guilt in his chest. He wasn't used to seeing the normally confident woman so off-balance. But as a bout of nerves buzzed around inside his gut, he realized he was feeling just as uneasy in her presence.

"So," Mona began. "You're probably wondering why I'm here."

Dillon folded his hands on top of the desk.

Don't crack, he told himself. *Make her sweat. Ask her why she stopped by unannounced. And uninvited.*

But when he looked into her soft, seemingly remorseful gaze, he backed down.

"I am curious. My guess is that you're here to report some sort of breaking news?"

"Actually, I am."

"Really?" he asked, scratching his jaw. "I was only kidding."

"Well, I'm not."

Dillon scooted farther into his desk, watching as Mona dug around inside her tote bag. She pulled out a piece of paper and slid it toward him.

"I just met with Olivia's coworker, Bonnie. She's been working to close out Olivia's files, and found some suspicious information on Alnico Aluminum Corporation."

Dillon skimmed the paper's contents. "And what is this?"

"An email from one of Alnico's executives. George Williamson. Apparently, he'd heard that Olivia was preparing to file a report with the government that contained damaging information against the company."

"I actually know George. He's a good guy. I met him through the community service initiatives he's sponsored in conjunction with the police department."

"Yeah, well, there may be two sides to Mr. Williamson. According to Olivia's file, Alnico had been illegally dumping hazardous waste into residential water sources. George tried to meet with her before she reported her findings. She refused, since that's against company policy. Then less than a week later, she goes missing."

"Hmm, interesting…"

Dillon ran his hand down his goatee as he read Olivia's response to George's meeting request. Then suddenly, he dropped the paper and looked up at Mona.

"Hold on. Alnico Aluminum Corporation is located right outside of Beechtree."

"I know. The very same area where Olivia went missing while she was collecting water samples. Coincidence? Maybe not."

Dillon jumped up from behind his desk, grabbing his keys and cell phone.

"Do you think you could get me a copy of that Alnico file?" he asked.

"I don't know. But I can ask Bonnie."

"Good. You do that. In the meantime, I need to get down to Alnico and talk to George. Find out where he was the day Olivia went missing."

Mona hopped up from her chair and followed Dillon out of his office.

"Wait," she said. "Shouldn't I go with you?"

Dillon stopped abruptly, right outside of Chief Boyer's office.

"I, um—I think I'd better partner up with a fellow law enforcement officer on this one."

"But I'm the one who gave you the lead," Mona insisted, taking a step closer to him. "I didn't have to do that. I could've gone straight to Alnico with my camera crew and questioned George myself. But I didn't."

"And you shouldn't have. Now listen, I appreciate you doing the right thing by turning this information over to me. But…" Dillon paused, struggling to find the right words. "I just don't want things to go left again like they did during Blake's interview."

"So that's where we're at now? You're gonna keep hanging that over my head instead of forgiving me and moving forward?"

"Come on, Mona. It's not like that. My initial conversation with George should be official police business. I don't want him thinking I'm trying to ambush him with a bunch of media madness. This needs to be taken seriously."

As soon as the words were out of his mouth, Dillon regretted speaking them.

A veil of darkness clouded Mona's eyes. The pain in her steely expression was apparent.

"Wait," he said, "I didn't mean it like—"

"Oh, I know exactly how you meant it," she interrupted. "So now you don't take me seriously? I'll have you know that I—"

"Hey!" Chief Boyer barked from inside his office. "I'm trying to watch a recording of the mayor's speech from last night. What's going on out there?"

Mona brushed past Dillon and stormed into his office.

"Chief," she huffed, "I just turned over a great piece of evidence to Dillon regarding Olivia's investigation."

"About?" Chief Boyer asked.

"It involves an executive at Alnico Aluminum who was illegally dumping waste into residential water sources. He requested a meeting with Olivia that she turned down, then shortly thereafter she went missing. I think I should accompany Detective Reed when he goes in to question him."

Chief Boyer sighed deeply, pausing the video he'd been watching. "Okay, so what's the problem, Detective?"

"Sir, while I am very appreciative of Mona's tip, I think it'd be best if I go down to Alnico and question George Williamson without her."

"Wait, George *Williamson*?" the chief asked, appearing perplexed as he rocked back in his chair. "Wow. I'm surprised to hear that. He's always come across as such a stand-up guy. So you two are thinking that he could be involved in Olivia's disappearance?"

"Yes," Mona replied. "He may have wanted to offer up some sort of bribe, or even threaten Olivia so she wouldn't report her findings to the government."

"Whatever the case may be," Dillon added, "I'd like to hear what he has to say for himself—"

"Yeah, so would I," Mona interjected.

Both she and Dillon stood rigidly in Chief Boyer's doorway, waiting to hear his verdict.

"I'd definitely like to hear what he has to say for himself." The chief glanced over at Dillon. "Are you sure you don't wanna bring him down to the station for questioning?"

"I'd rather not. I don't want him to think he's being detained. I'd like for him to feel comfortable. Or as comfortable as he can while being questioned by a detective about his involvement in a missing person case."

"Good idea," Chief Boyer replied. "You know what else I think would be a good idea?"

"What's that, sir?"

"For you to take Mona with you."

"Yes," Dillon heard her hiss underneath her breath. He ignored Mona and remained focused on his boss.

"But, Chief, hasn't there already been enough damage done to compromise this investigation? I'd like to maintain the last bits of its integrity."

"Hey, I take offense to that," Mona shot back.

"Look, I'm just speaking the truth, and—"

"Listen!" Chief Boyer interrupted, silencing them both. "You two need to pull it together. Now, Detective

Reed, I've said it before and I'll say it again. Mona's reputation speaks for itself. Her involvement in any case is advantageous."

"Thank you," she slipped in.

"But," the chief continued, eyeing Mona directly, "while you have certainly been an asset to this investigation, you've also had a few…*mishaps*. I'm expecting that won't happen again."

Dillon glanced over at Mona, noticing that her satisfied smirk had transformed into a slight frown.

"No. It won't happen again, sir," she muttered.

"Good. Now, I recommended this partnership between you two for good reason. Reed, your detective skills are bar none. You don't miss. You're a patient, quiet storm who knows exactly when to move in on a suspect and make an arrest."

"Thanks, Chief."

"And, Mona, your people skills, instincts and attention to detail are invaluable. No other evidence was discovered near the Beechtree water source where Olivia allegedly went missing, except for the necklace you found. Did you know that?"

"Yes," she chirped. "I did."

Dillon could see her peering over at him through the corner of his eye. He ignored her.

"Together," Chief Boyer continued, "I have no doubt that you two will get this case solved. So get down to Alnico and find out what George has to say for himself. And hey, leave through the back door so that the reporters out front won't try to stop you with a barrage of questions."

"Good idea," Dillon replied. "We'll report back to you once we're done."

"Great. And I'm expecting you two will behave yourselves."

"Of course, Chief," Mona assured him.

Dillon stepped to the side and held out his arm.

"After you," he said to her.

She slinked past him, remaining silent while walking toward the back of the station. He followed closely behind her.

"You probably want to ride in separate cars," Mona said when they exited the building. "So I'll just meet you in front of Alnico."

"Don't be ridiculous. I can drive us both there."

"Really?" Mona asked, her staunch poker face softening.

"Yes. Really. Now come on. Let's go and speak with George."

Chapter Thirteen

Mona could feel her blood pumping rapidly through her veins as she followed Dillon inside Alnico Aluminum Corporation.

The company's corporate offices were located across the street from the manufacturing plant. The vast lobby's floor-to-ceiling windows surrounded beautiful black-and-white marble floors. Sleek white leather furniture sat among modern steel-and-glass coffee tables. Pricey abstract artwork hung from the walls, and a massive, glossy white reception desk covered the back wall.

"Wow," Mona murmured. "Looks like a lot of Alnico's multibillion-dollar annual revenue went into decorating this lobby."

"It sure does," Dillon agreed.

Mona felt her tense muscles relax a bit after hearing his response. She was worried that he'd be annoyed after Chief Boyer forced him to bring her along to question George.

Just stay in your lane, she reminded herself. *Don't take over the conversation. Let Dillon take the lead...*

"May I help you?" she heard a woman ask haughtily from behind the reception desk.

Mona stayed back, allowing Dillon to approach her.

"Good afternoon. My name is Detective Reed. I'm here to see George Williamson. Is he available?"

"Is Mr. Williamson expecting you?"

Mona peered over Dillon's shoulder. The woman sitting behind the desk looked more like a model than a receptionist. Her long, bone-straight blond hair was slicked back into a severe ponytail. Beautiful translucent makeup covered her flawless porcelain skin. Her perfectly tailored jade green jumpsuit could've been taken straight off the runway, as could her snooty expression.

"No," Dillon replied, "he isn't expecting me. But I'm here on official police business and would like to ask him a few questions."

He eyed the receptionist as she remained silent, staring back at him.

Mona balled her hands into tight fists. Her palms burned with discomfort. She shifted her weight from right to left, wondering whether she should say something.

No! she told herself. *Do not overstep your bounds. Dillon can handle it.*

"I'm sorry," the receptionist finally said. "But Mr. Williamson isn't available right now."

"How do you know?" Dillon asked, his patient tone tinged with sprinkles of irritation. "You didn't even call him."

"I don't have to. I'm aware of his schedule and know that he is not able to speak with you at this time."

Mona cleared her throat, unable to hold back any longer. She stepped up from behind Dillon and approached the desk.

"Hello," she purred while smiling sweetly. "I'm Mona Avery. And you are?"

The receptionist gasped so loudly that the sound reverberated through the lobby. She hopped up from her chair and offered Mona her hand.

"I'm—I'm Em-Emily. Emily Bradford," the young woman stammered. "And I am so sorry, Ms. Avery. I had no idea that you were here with this man."

"Detective Reed," he interjected.

"Yeah, okay," Emily said without taking her eyes off Mona. "Ms. Avery, I am your biggest fan. I'm in graduate school right now studying journalism in hopes that I could one day have a career half as successful as yours."

"Aw," Mona said while firmly shaking her hand. "That is so kind of you. Thank you. I have no doubt that you will one day have a career ten times more successful than mine."

"Ha!" Emily snorted. "I seriously doubt that. But thank you for the vote of confidence. I will carry those words with me always."

Take advantage of this moment, Mona thought to herself. *Go in for the kill...*

"So you said that Mr. Williamson isn't available, huh?" she asked. "Are you sure about that?"

Emily's eyes widened. She glanced around the lobby, holding her hand to her chest as she tiptoed around the desk.

Mona almost jumped back when the receptionist grabbed her arm and pulled her in close.

"Mr. Williamson isn't here," Emily whispered. "I don't know what's going on, but I've heard rumblings that after your *incredible* interview with Blake Carter, he skipped town."

"He *skipped town*?" Mona asked. "But…why? And where did he go?"

"After the way you interrogated Blake on national television, Mr. Williamson felt as though he might be next because of a report Olivia Whitman was getting ready to file against Alnico. So he fled to the Bahamas in hopes that everything would blow over soon."

"Do you have any idea when he's planning to return to Lake Landry?" Dillon asked.

Emily shot him a look of annoyance, as if he were intruding on a private conversation between her and Mona.

"No," she chirped, "I don't. But if Ms. Avery would like for me to find that information out for her, I'm sure I could."

"You could?" Mona asked, pressing her hands against her cheeks for added shock value. "For *me*?"

"Of course I could," Emily gushed. "Anything for you…"

"Oh boy," Mona heard Dillon sigh underneath his breath.

Don't be a hater, Mona wanted to tell him. But instead she pulled a business card from her bag and handed it to Emily.

"Here's my contact information," she told her. "Please feel free to reach out to me once you find out when Mr. Williamson will be back in town."

"Because I'm guessing he's completely off the grid and unreachable via phone or email," Dillon interjected.

"Of course he is," Emily shot back before turning her attention to Mona.

"Anyway, just between us, I may be able to get more information about Mr. Williamson. I'm really close with his executive assistant. So I'll see if I can dig around and find anything that might be pertinent to the investigation. If I do, I'll contact you."

"Emily," Mona sighed. "You are an absolute gem. Thank you. And, hey, why don't you send me your résumé. Maybe you can come out to LA and intern at CNB News next summer."

"What?" the receptionist squealed, jumping up and down while rapidly clapping her hands. "That would be so amazing! You'll have my résumé in your inbox later this afternoon."

"I look forward to reviewing it. Thanks for that exclusive scoop, Emily. Consider this moment your first experience in investigative journalism."

Mona gave her a wink and a wave, then spun around and headed toward the exit. She could hear Dillon shuffling behind her.

"Bye, Ms. Avery!" Emily called out. "So nice meeting you!"

"Same here!"

Mona stepped to the side as Dillon opened the door for her. The minute they reached the parking lot, she turned to him with a huge grin on her face.

"Don't even say it," he huffed. "I am not in the mood to hear any sort of gloating right now."

"Me? Gloat? Why I take great offense to that, Detective Reed."

"Get in the car," he said, opening the passenger door before chuckling softly.

"Not until you tell me how much of an asset I am to this investigation."

"Oh, now you're pushing it, Avery. Get me some solid evidence from your new best friend Emily, then maybe I'll consider it. But in the meantime, how about I treat you to lunch? I've had a taste for grilled bourbon chicken from the Cajun Cookout Café all week."

"Mmm, that sounds delicious," Mona replied. "I am a little full, though, after I devoured your pathetic little attempt to talk to George in there."

"Please get in the car, woman!" Dillon insisted before both he and Mona burst out laughing.

The twosome climbed inside and headed out of the parking lot toward the restaurant.

"Oh, before I forget," Mona began, "I did reach out to Bonnie and ask if she could send me the full file on Alnico."

"What'd she say?"

"I haven't heard back from her yet. Which is weird considering how eager she's been to help out with the investigation."

Dillon shrugged his shoulders. "Who knows. Maybe she's been busy after taking on Olivia's workload. Just keep trying."

"I will."

He glanced over at Mona. "Listen. You've definitely been an asset to this investigation. A huge one. And... I owe you an apology. I shouldn't have just cut you off like that after Blake's interview. He was completely out of line and acted like an arrogant ass. I could've been more understanding of your reaction."

"Thank you for that, Dillon. And again, I apologize, too. I shouldn't have let Blake get me to the point where I compromised the investigation. Now all this media is swarming around town, sensationalizing the case. It's exactly what you *didn't* want to happen."

"Yeah, well, we're moving on from it, right? We've

got this new lead with George Williamson, and I've still got my eye on Blake. Things are definitely looking up with this case."

"Yes, they are."

Mona watched Dillon closely. He appeared so content, as if he were happy she was there. She resisted the urge to lean over and kiss his soft lips as they spread into a slight smile.

The moment was interrupted when Dillon's cell phone buzzed. He stopped at a red light and tapped the screen.

"Oh no," he moaned.

"What's wrong?"

He turned to Mona, the color slowly draining from his face.

"Bonnie is dead."

Chapter Fourteen

Mona sat straight up, raising her chin as the producer adjusted her mic.

She glanced around The Bayou Inn's modest conference room. It's where she'd decided to hold Oliver's interview, which they finally scheduled after he saw her sit down with Blake and insisted on clearing his name live on air.

The festive Christmas decorations that had been hung around the room were replaced by dark backdrops. Mona was seated in one of four black mesh ergonomic chairs surrounding a small round cherrywood table. Her production crew was busy setting up their equipment while Mona's stylist touched up her hair and makeup.

It had been a week since Bonnie's body was found floating in Rosehill Park's lily pond. She'd been shot in the back of the head. There was little evidence found at the crime scene, and no suspects were in custody.

The sinister turn in the investigation had shaken Mona to her core. But she was determined to press on until the case was solved.

Mona took a deep breath and straightened the hem on her navy blue silk wrap dress.

"Any word from Oliver?" her producer, Sarah, asked.

"We're going live in fifteen minutes and I need to get him prepped and mic'd up."

"He texted me at three o'clock this morning confirming that he'd be here."

"And you haven't heard from him since?"

"No, I haven't. But I'll send him a message and find out what time he'll be—"

Before Mona could finish, Oliver came bursting inside the conference room.

"I made it!" he announced, holding his arms out at his sides as if he were waiting on a round of applause. He almost dropped the extra large coffee cup he was holding in his hand. "Let the phenomenon of my voice being heard all around the world begin."

Mona resisted the urge to roll her eyes.

"Good morning, Oliver," she said, struggling to sound pleasant as she motioned him over. "I'm glad you're here. This is Sarah, my show's producer. She'll be getting you mic'd up. My cameraman, Steve, is adjusting the lighting. Would you like for my makeup artist, Megan, to apply a little concealer under your eyes or dust a bit of powder across your T-zone?"

"What, and hide all this handsomeness?" he deadpanned. "No, thanks. I came here looking exactly how I want to appear on camera."

Mona stared at Oliver through the corner of her eye. He was dressed decently enough in a mustard yellow sweater and jeans that weren't ripped throughout.

But it appeared as though he'd made no attempt to tame his unkempt curly hair or trim his scruffy beard.

His eyes were bloodshot red, a clear indication that he'd been up all night. And he was jittery. Between the caffeine and his adrenaline, he could barely stand still.

"You're going to take a seat right here." Sarah pointed, directing Oliver to the chair across from Mona's.

"Got it," he said, plopping down so hard that the wheels gave way. It tilted dangerously onto its right-side legs.

He gripped the edge of the table for dear life, barely avoiding crashing to the floor.

Mona reached out and clutched his arm. "Are you okay?"

"Yep! I'm good. Just a little wired, I guess. I'll be all right once we get started."

Oliver bounced anxiously in his seat, tapping his fingernails against the table.

"So where's your boy, Detective Rivers?" he asked.

"*Reed.* He's on his way. Had a few things to take care of down at the police station."

"*Tuh!* You mean he had to shuffle a few papers around on his desk?"

Mona ignored the snide comment, refusing to let Oliver take her out of interview mode.

She took a deep breath and glanced down at her questions, then jumped at the sound of his booming voice.

"There's the man of the hour!" he roared.

Mona looked up at the doorway. Her chest pounded at the sight of Dillon swaggering into the room.

"Hello, everyone," he said.

His presence immediately put Mona at ease.

She was surprised to see him dressed in a slim-fitting charcoal gray suit, crisp white shirt and black cap-toe Oxford shoes. She'd never seen Dillon look so handsome.

"Hello, Detective Reed," she said, struggling to keep her voice steady. "You're right on time. We were just about to get started."

"Good. Glad I wasn't late. I'll just take a seat over here in the corner and let you and Oliver do your thing."

"Thanks, Detective Rivers," Oliver quipped.

"Reed," Dillon shot back.

"Are we ready to get started?" Sarah asked.

"I'm ready," Mona responded. "How are you feeling now, Oliver? A little calmer?"

"Not really. But last night's tarot card reading confirmed that all would go well today. My seven chakras are perfectly aligned. And I'm depending on the universe to guide my words. So I'm good. Let's do this."

She stared across the table at Oliver as he took a huge gulp from his coffee cup. She had no idea what he was talking about and knew not to ask for clarification.

Lord, please don't let this interview go left...

"Okay, everyone, quiet please," Sarah said. "Going live in five, four, three, two…"

She pointed at Mona, who looked directly into the camera with a stoic expression on her face.

"Hello, everyone. Thank you for joining me during this special broadcast. In my continued effort to assist Lake Landry's law enforcement agency in finding Olivia Whitman, I have her twin brother, Oliver Whitman, here with me today. Oliver, thank you for agreeing to speak with me."

"Ah, it's cool. Thanks for having me. And for giving me a platform to speak my truth."

"Oliver, what do you think happened to your sister?"

"I don't know." He shrugged nonchalantly. "You're

the expert, aren't you? What do *you* think happened to her?"

Mona froze. The response caught her by surprise. She clenched her jaws together tightly, searching her brain for a quick comeback.

"Well, I've got my theories," she replied. "But as someone so close to her, I brought you here today hoping you could share your thoughts with viewers. Maybe provide some insight into what was going on in Olivia's life shortly before she went missing."

"First of all, my sister and I aren't close. And you know that, because you've been in our lives since we were teenagers. Secondly, Olivia and I didn't talk on a regular basis. So I have no idea what was going on in her life before she went missing."

Mona just sat there, staring at Oliver in disbelief. She couldn't believe he'd come onto her show just to waste everyone's time with his short, vapid answers.

I should've listened to Dillon. I never should have gone live on air with this man.

"But I will say this," Oliver continued. "Things between Olivia and her husband, Blake Carter, were *not* good."

Mona perked up after hearing the comment.

Thank you for giving me something to work with! she almost yelled.

"What do you mean, things weren't good between them? Can you please elaborate on that?"

"Well, I worked at Transformation Cosmetics for a while before that *jerk* Leo Mendez fired me. While I was there, I'd see Blake fawning all over women around the office. I heard he was partaking in intimate lunches behind closed doors that didn't just entail eating food, if you know what I mean. Olivia heard about all that, too."

"Was she planning on leaving Blake?"

"That's what I heard. But before she could? *Boom!* She goes missing. Suspicious, wouldn't you say?"

"It's definitely an interesting coincidence," Mona responded, careful not to allow Oliver to bait her. "But while there's no denying that Blake is a philanderer, that doesn't make him a criminal."

"True. And Olivia isn't innocent in all this either. There are reasons why Blake couldn't stay faithful to a flawed woman like her."

Mona felt her stomach drop.

Do not let this interview go off the rails...

"But Olivia is our victim here. We need to be respectful of—"

"Respectful?" Oliver interrupted. "Please. I'd show some respect had Olivia not married Blake in the first place. She never really loved him, you know. How could she? He always treated her like crap! But Olivia is greedy. Money and power hungry. And—"

"Oliver," Mona interrupted, "we're getting off track here. This isn't about—"

"Excuse me, let me finish! You asked me to sit down with you so that I could share my take on Olivia's disappearance. Now please, allow me to do that."

"Can you do so without attacking her character?"

Oliver's lips twisted into a snarky smirk.

"I'll try. Anyway, my sister is more concerned about her image than love. Marrying into the Carter family was a good look for her. While we Whitmans can hold our own when it comes to big bank accounts, joining forces with the Carters took Olivia's status to a whole 'nother level. And being the superficial bi—*woman* that she is, my sister loved that prestige."

A wave of heat washed over Mona. Droplets of sweat covered her back. She was tempted to cut the interview short. But they were live. So she had to keep going.

"Oliver," Mona said calmly, "Olivia and I have been very good friends for years. The woman you're describing is far from the woman I know. Olivia is kind and loving. She cares a great deal for her husband. She wanted their marriage to work. It's never been about money for her, which is why she worked so hard to earn a master's degree in environmental science and land a job at LLL Water Quality Laboratory."

"Another power play, if you ask me," Oliver snorted. "Olivia's position at LLL gives her the authority to shut companies down if she sees fit."

"Do you think that authority might have had something to do with her disappearance?"

"Who knows. It could. Or maybe it's Olivia's karma coming back to bite her in the ass."

Oh, please don't go there...

"As one of my fellow conspiracy theorists," Oliver continued, pointing across the table at Mona, "you believe in kismet, don't you? The idea that whatever is meant to be, will be?"

She nodded her head, remaining silent to discourage one of his rants.

"You can't be greedy," he rambled, "and marry a man for money rather than love, and think it's not gonna come back to haunt you. Oh! And let's not forget the fact that Olivia knew Blake wanted children. He'd been talking about starting a family ever since the day they met. But once he married her? *Bam!* She refused to give the man children!"

Mona glanced over at Dillon, who had a pained expression on his face. She could just feel the words *I told you so* coming off him.

"Let me ask you a question," she said to Oliver, desperate to take the interview in a different direction. "I recently conducted an interview with Olivia's husband, Blake. Did you happen to see it?"

"Yes, I did."

"In it, he admitted to his infidelity. He also alleged that you and Olivia have a complicated family history, and you may have had something to do with Olivia's disappearance. What do you have to say to that?"

Oliver ran his hands rigorously over his ratty beard. When he failed to answer the question, Mona kept going.

"Why would you sit here and defend a man who'd say those things about you, all while slamming your own sister's character? You're in essence blaming her for her own disappearance."

"Look, don't get me wrong. I can't stand Blake Carter. But he and my sister were in a messed-up relationship. Because of that, I'm thinking maybe she pulled a *Gone Girl*–type of stunt on the world and disappeared on her own accord."

"Which is the conspiracy theorist in you."

"Possibly," Oliver said. "But it's plausible that Olivia faked her own kidnapping in hopes of getting some attention, which we all know she loves, and framing her husband out of spite. She could very well be exacting revenge on the man who broke his vows and publicly humiliated her."

"Let's switch gears for a minute here, Oliver. There's been a buzz around Lake Landry for years about your place in the Whitman family. It's been said that you're bitter toward Olivia and your parents. That you feel like a stepchild rather than a full-fledged member of the family. Is there any truth to that?"

Oliver's expression fell into a rumpled frown. He folded his arms in front of him, rocking back and forth in his chair.

"Hell yeah there's some truth to that," he spat. "Olivia gets treated like a princess. And me? Like a pauper. She has everything. The money, the big house, the big job, the prominent husband. What do I have? *Nothing.* I'm stuck getting mistreated by my parents, who don't even *try* to understand my elevated level of brilliance."

"Then why don't you move out of your parents' house and stand on your own two feet, Oliver? Get a job. Take care of yourself so you won't have to worry about being mistreated."

He slammed his hands down onto the table.

"Because it's not that easy for me, Mona! These people out here can't comprehend my celestial existence. I get ostracized for simply being supreme. But that's okay. Just know that once I collect my half of the Whitman family fortune, which I hope will be sooner rather than later, this world will see what Oliver Bernard Whitman is made of."

Mona's head swiveled at his callous statement.

"Wait, are you actually wishing your parents an early demise so that you can collect your inheritance?"

"I said what I said," Oliver replied defiantly. "Interpret it however you see fit."

"Wow," Mona murmured, pausing while glancing down at her notes. She needed a moment to regroup.

"Maybe if Olivia doesn't resurface," he continued, "I'll get her half of the inheritance, as well."

Mona fumbled her papers, almost dropping them to the floor.

"Oliver, please. I know you don't mean that."

"Oh, I totally mean it. And since I'm being honest here, I might as well admit that my life has been *so* peaceful since Olivia went missing. In fact, I'm actually glad she's gone. And I hope she never comes back."

Mona's mouth fell open. She stared across the table, trembling at the sight of Oliver's dark, lifeless eyes.

When she turned to Sarah to ask if they could cut to commercial, the Whitmans came bursting through the door.

"Oliver!" Mrs. Whitman yelled. "What in the hell do you think you're doing?"

"Airing out this family, *finally*," he defiantly replied. "I'm done living the Whitman lie. Acting like all is well when it's not. The world deserves to know that you two treat your only son like crap."

"You're a fool!" Mr. Whitman shouted before lunging at his son.

Dillon jumped up from his chair. He grabbed hold of Oliver's father right before his fist connected with his son's jaw.

"Keep rolling!" Mona heard Sarah tell their cameraman.

"Steve, no!" Mona insisted. "Stop the camera. Now!"

"Yes, ma'am," he replied, immediately ending the recording.

Dillon continued to hold Mr. Whitman back as Oliver pulled out his cell phone and began recording the confrontation.

"This is gonna blow my social media *up!*" he exclaimed, laughing while Dillon struggled to detain his father.

"Oliver, I cannot believe you would betray your own family like this," Mrs. Whitman cried. "How could you say such horrible things about your sister?"

"Mom, let's face it. Olivia is a bitch. And I stated nothing but the facts about this family—"

"Oliver!" Dillon barked. "That's enough. Steve, can you please escort him out of here while I stay back with his parents?"

"I don't need nobody to escort me outta here," Oliver insisted, his wild eyes darting around the room. "I get it. I'm probably America's most wanted right now. But it's all good. At least I'm living in my truth. Unlike all you phonies. Peace out."

Oliver strutted toward the conference room door. Mona just stood there in a state of shock. She peered over at Dillon, who was busy consoling the Whitmans.

Her eyes filled with tears. She couldn't decide which interview had been worse, Oliver's or Blake's.

"What did you do to my daughter?" Mrs. Whitman whimpered at Oliver as he strolled out the door. "What did you do to my daughter?"

He turned around and aimed his camera at her.

"Aw, look at my mom," he said. "Hey, to all my followers out there, just know that this is the most attention my parents have given me in *years*. Years!"

"Cut that damn camera off and answer your mother's question!" Mr. Whitman yelled.

"Go to hell, Dad. See you all at home!"

Mr. Whitman balled his fists as he struggled to compose himself.

Mrs. Whitman turned to Mona and glared at her.

"How could you do this? Betray our family like this? You knew Oliver was in no condition to be interviewed live on television. Yet you did it anyway, exploiting the Whitman name for the sake of ratings. You should be ashamed of yourself."

"I—I, um…" she stammered. "But Oliver approached me asking if I'd provide him with a platform to speak after Blake's interview aired."

"I don't care!" Mrs. Whitman argued. "You and Detective Reed both witnessed how unstable Oliver is after I opened up my home to you."

"And what did you do with that information?" Mr. Whitman added. "The complete opposite of what you *should* have. See, this is exactly why we wanted to keep Olivia's disappearance out of the media and take care of matters privately."

Mona bit the inside of her jaw, struggling not to burst into tears.

"Mr. and Mrs. Whitman, please know that my only goal is to help find Olivia. That's all I want."

"No, you want ratings," Mr. Whitman told her. "And notoriety. Whatever positive traits you picked up during your time here in Lake Landry are long gone, young lady. You've obviously been corrupted by the underbelly of Hollywood."

"That is not true," Mona whispered, her raspy voice trembling with pain. "Everything I do is done with integrity. And I agreed to conduct this interview with the best intentions."

Mrs. Whitman turned her nose up at her. "Well, as

the saying goes, the road to hell is paved with good intentions. Detective Reed, could you please see to it that my husband and I get back to our home safely?"

"Of course."

Dillon followed the Whitmans toward the door. But his eyes were glued to Mona. When he mouthed the words *I'll call you*, she nodded her head and began gathering her things.

"I need to get out of here and get some air," Mona told her production crew. "Can you all wrap everything up and see yourselves out?"

"Of course," Sarah said without looking up from her phone. "We'll take it from here. And hey, I know you may not wanna hear this right now, but CNB News's social media platforms are on fire. According to the PR team, the website crashed after viewers hit the comment section."

"But it's up and running again," Steve, who was also scrolling through his phone, chimed in. "And boy oh boy, have the tables turned."

"What do you mean?" Mona asked.

Her makeup artist, Megan, who was peeking at Steve's phone over his shoulder, gasped loudly while jumping up and down.

"What is going on?" Mona asked, grabbing her own cell and pulling up CNB's website.

"Welp, according to this poll CNB took, everybody now thinks that Oliver is behind Olivia's disappearance. *Not* Blake."

"So Blake is no longer public enemy number one?" Sarah asked.

"Nope," Steve said. "Oliver Whitman is officially the nation's new suspect."

All eyes turned to Mona.

"Ugh," she moaned, tossing her phone inside her purse and grabbing her things. "This is insane. I cannot believe yet another one of my interviews turned into a complete disaster."

"But look at all the attention you're bringing to this case," Sarah told her. "And the viewership you're bringing to CNB News."

"I don't care about the viewership, Sarah! My reputation is on the line here, and more importantly, Olivia's safety. I'm trying to run a reputable news program, not some sensational trash show. Between Blake's interview and now Oliver's, that's exactly what my broadcast has become."

"Well, call it what you want," Sarah quipped. "Whatever you're doing is working, because according to your boss, your show just received the highest ratings in CNB's history."

Mona rolled her eyes and waved Sarah off.

"Under normal circumstances," she began, "hearing that would've been music to my ears. But after tonight? I couldn't care less. And with that being said, I have got to get out of here. I'll call you all tomorrow."

Mona hurried out of the conference room just as tears began to stream down her face.

MONA SAT ALONE on the inn's back deck, sipping a glass of much-needed red wine.

It had been a couple of hours since her interview with Oliver. Even though her phone had been buzzing nonstop, she refused to respond to most of the texts, emails and phone calls.

The one message she did check was Dillon's. He

was still with the Whitmans, trying to convince them that they'd get to the bottom of Olivia's disappearance after they threatened to contact the FBI and a private investigator.

Mona asked if he could come by once he was done. She wasn't in the mood to be alone. He said he'd be there as soon as he could.

She drained her glass and set it down on the table. She slipped off her shoes, then walked out onto the lawn.

The soft, cool grass felt good underneath her bare soles. She dragged her feet through the thick turf, walking farther into the darkness.

Mona was overcome by a sense of peace. The calm, wooded area hidden behind the inn helped soothe her rattled nerves. She sauntered farther toward the dense brush, inhaling the aromatic scent of pine needles.

Just when she thought she'd heard tree branches rustling in the distance, Mona's cell phone buzzed. She pulled it from her pocket. A text message notification from Dillon appeared on the screen.

Hey. Wrapping things up with the Whitmans now. Finally got them to calm down and convinced them to give us a little more time to solve this case. The fact that Oliver isn't here definitely made things easier. I'll be there as soon as I can.

"Thank goodness," Mona muttered to herself as she composed a response.

Good. Glad you were able to buy us more time. After Oliver's interview, I definitely think we need to take a closer look at him. I can't believe the things he said about his own sister. We have a lot to discuss. See you soon.

Right before Mona sent the message, she heard what sounded like someone rustling through the trees.

That's when she realized she was not alone.

Mona spun around and shot off toward the inn. Twigs that had fallen from the trees sliced at her feet. She ignored the pain, determined to get to safety.

When shallow puffs of air failed to fill her constricting lungs, she choked. The lack of oxygen slowed her down.

She could feel a dark presence looming behind her. The predator was getting closer.

She ran as fast as she could. A gust of humid wind propelled her forward. When the tips of her toes got caught underneath a jagged branch, Mona stumbled.

She fell forward, plunging to the damp ground.

Her attacker pounced.

She tried to scream out when his heavy body landed on top of hers. But she couldn't eke out more than a feeble wheeze.

Mona parted her lips, once again attempting to scream. But he quickly covered her mouth with his dry, salty hand.

She bit down on his fingers, jumping at the startling sound of his animalistic growl.

"You *bitch*!" he grunted, mushing her facedown into the mud.

Mona struggled to catch a pocket of breath. A clump of dirt slipped inside her mouth. She forced her head out of the mud and spit it out.

"Who are you?" she cried. "Why are you doing this to me?"

The prowler grabbed a handful of her hair, pulling her ear close to his lips.

"We've been over this before, Mona. I'm doing this to you because you *refuse* to back off of the Olivia Whitman investigation. How many times do I have to warn you before I have to kill you? Olivia is not your concern. Why would you want to die over something that has nothing to do with you?"

Olivia is my concern! Mona wanted to yell. But when she felt the cold, hard end of a gun dig into her temple, she remained silent.

"Now, you listen to me," the attacker hissed, "and listen to me good. Go back inside that inn, pack your bags and get the hell out of Lake Landry. *Immediately.* Do you understand me?"

Before Mona could respond, she heard the gun cock. *You cannot let this man take your life. Fight back!*

"Do you *understand* me?" the attacker repeated, more forcefully this time.

Mona frantically ran her hand along the ground until it landed on a rock. She grabbed it, reached back and slammed her assailant against the side of his head.

"Aaah!" he yelled.

Her attacker rolled over, gripping his temple while moaning in pain.

Mona quickly pushed herself up onto her knees. *The gun. Get the gun!*

She reached down and grabbed the firearm.

He tightened his grip, then swung his fist toward her eye.

Mona ducked, barely avoiding the blow. She dug her

fingernails into his hand, hoping the pain would release his grasp on the gun.

It didn't.

"You think you can get the best of me?" he grunted. "It'll never happen. You're too weak!"

"*I'm* weak? Correction. *You're* weak! You've been trying to kill me since I got to Lake Landry. It hasn't happened yet, and it's not about to happen now!"

Mona bent down, preparing to sink her teeth into the assailant's hand. And then...

Boom!

The gun went off.

Mona screamed, falling backward as the sound of the bullet ricocheted through the air.

She stared over at her attacker. He wasn't moving. But he was still holding the gun.

She leaned forward, checking to see whether he'd been shot.

"Gotcha!" he yelled, lunging toward her.

Mona quickly rolled over to the side. He landed on the ground, missing her by inches.

Just as she scrambled to her feet, the sound of a car engine roared in the near distance.

Headlights flashed across the darkness. Tires screeched over rough gravel.

Dillon!

When the headlights went out and a car door slammed, Mona's attacker began to crawl away.

Go after him. Get a look at him. Bite him. Scratch him. Get his DNA. Call out to Dillon. Do something!

But she was too afraid. Her assailant still had the gun in his possession.

Just stay calm. Help is on the way.

"I think she's still out on the back deck," Mona heard Evelyn say.

"Okay, cool," Dillon replied. "I'll meet her out there."

The inn's back door opened. Mona's attacker jumped to his feet and ran off into the darkness.

"Dillon!" Mona screamed out from the lawn.

"Mona? Where are you?"

"Out here!"

She struggled to walk toward him. Her wobbly legs could barely hold her up.

"Mona!" Dillon once again called out. "I don't see you!"

She opened her mouth to speak, but only managed to muster up a lingering sob.

The thumping of Dillon's footsteps drew near. Mona looked up and saw him hurrying toward her. She was overcome by a wave of relief.

"What happened to you?" he asked.

Mona responded by falling into his arms.

"Hey, hey," he murmured, gently embracing her. "It's okay. I'm here now. Come on. Let's get you inside."

She didn't budge. She gripped Dillon's back while crying into his chest. "I was attacked again."

"You were *what*?"

"I was attacked again," Mona sobbed, her voice cracking.

"Oh no," he moaned, embracing her tighter. "How long ago did this happen?"

"Right before you got here. He fled after hearing you pull up."

Dillon reached down in his pocket and pulled out his cell phone, shining the flashlight around the vicinity.

"What are the chances he might still be in the area?"

"Not likely. He ran off into the woods several minutes ago. Plenty of time to get a good lead."

"My God," he muttered. "I bet you it was Oliver. He never showed up at his parents' house. I'm gonna call for backup. Have the area checked. You never know what we may find."

Mona sniffled loudly while pulling away from Dillon and wiping dirt from her face.

"Are you okay?" Dillon asked softly, placing his hands on Mona's arms. "Do you need to go to the hospital?"

"No. I'm fine. Even though the attack was pretty physical. He had me pinned to the ground with all of his body weight. But this time, he had a gun. Things are getting worse, Dillon. We have to solve this case. *Now.* Because if we don't, I might end up just like…"

Mona's voice trailed off. Angry tears streamed down her face. Her body shook at the thought of her assault. Visions of Olivia being attacked flashed through her mind.

"Listen," Dillon said, "I am so sorry this happened to you. Do you think it's time to consider going home and—"

"No! I've never been one to give up and I'm not about to start now. I am determined to stay in Lake Landry until I get justice for Olivia."

He sighed deeply, leading Mona back toward the inn. "I can understand that. I just can't help but feel responsible for this because once again, I wasn't here to protect you."

Mona slowly climbed up the deck's stairs and slipped on her sandals.

"This wasn't your fault, Dillon."

"Yeah, well, I feel otherwise. Now let's get you inside. You can give me the details of what happened tonight and I'll file a police report."

"And what about Oliver? What are you going to do about him?"

"I will definitely be bringing him down to the station for questioning."

"Good," Mona said, leaning into Dillon as they headed inside the inn.

Chapter Fifteen

Dillon glanced down at his watch. It was a quarter past five. Oliver was over an hour late.

He had arranged for Oliver to meet him down at the station the day after his disastrous interview for questioning. Considering he had yet to arrive, Dillon was ready to report him to Chief Boyer as a no-show.

Just as his cell phone buzzed, there was a knock at his office door.

"It's open!"

Chief Boyer cracked open the door and stuck his head inside.

"Hey, just checking in to see if you've heard from Oliver."

Dillon grabbed his cell and checked the home screen. The only new notification that appeared was a text message from Mona.

"Nope," he told the chief. "Not a peep."

"Have you tried his parents?"

"I have. Neither of them are answering their phones."

"Hmm…" Chief Boyer sighed. "Welp, I'll give it a shot and call the Whitmans. See if they know where he is. You may have to hit the streets and find him. If he refuses to come to you, then you may have to go to him."

"That's fine with me. And good luck trying to get ahold of his parents. After that interview, they see the writing on the wall. They probably don't want to face the fact that their own son may have something to do with his sister's disappearance."

"Who could blame them? I'd be devastated if I were in their shoes. Nevertheless, I'll try to reach out to them now."

"Thanks," Dillon said. "Let me know how it goes."

"Will do."

After the chief left his office, Dillon opened Mona's text message.

FYI, I just heard back from Emily at Alnico Aluminum. She didn't find any incriminating info in George Williamson's email account. She said she'll continue to keep an eye out for us. But at this point, I think you and I both know who's behind all this. Speaking of which, has Oliver come in for questioning yet?

No, not yet, he replied. I reached out to his parents to find out if they knew of his whereabouts, but didn't get an answer. Chief Boyer is contacting them now. Hopefully he'll have better luck—

Dillon's cell phone rang, interrupting his reply. It was Mona calling. He tapped the accept button.

"Hey," he said, "I was just responding to your message. Oliver isn't here yet, so Chief Boyer just went to call his parents—"

"Dillon!" Mona interrupted, her voice filled with panic. "Oliver has been attacked!"

"Wait, *what*?"

"Oliver has been attacked!" she screamed.

"Where? When? We haven't gotten any calls here at the station about an assault."

"That's because Oliver didn't call it in. He was severely beaten in his parents' driveway on the way to the station. The Whitmans heard all the commotion and ran outside to see what was going on. But by the time they'd gotten to him, the assailant had fled the scene."

"Similar to the way it happened to you," he noted.

"Exactly. But unlike my attacks, Oliver's injuries are pretty extensive."

"How do you know all this?" Dillon asked.

"Surprisingly, Mrs. Whitman called and told me. After she and Mr. Whitman got Oliver back inside the house, he insisted that they not call law enforcement and asked them to call me instead."

"Really? So they're not mad about the whole interview debacle anymore?"

"I guess not," Mona sighed. "I asked Mrs. Whitman if I could come by and talk to Oliver."

"What'd she say?"

"She said yes. And of course I asked if you could come with me."

Dillon felt a pounding inside his chest as he waited for Mona to continue. When she didn't, his jaws clenched in frustration.

"She said no, huh."

"Well…she didn't say no. But she didn't say yes either. I think she's worried that Oliver may get upset seeing you there. She mentioned him rambling something about the attack being set up by the police. And he thinks Blake is paying off law enforcement, too."

"Good grief," Dillon muttered, dropping his head

in his hand. "Oliver and his conspiracy theories. This entire investigation is getting more and more twisted by the day."

"That it is. I think you should just take your chances and come to the house with me. At this point, we don't have anything to lose. Up until Oliver's interview, I'd had a feeling that he held the key in helping us solve this case. Now that he's been attacked, I'm almost certain of it."

Dillon stood up and grabbed his keys. "I have to agree with you there. Did Mrs. Whitman happen to mention whether Oliver needs medical attention?"

"She did. Despite Oliver's objections, the family doctor is there now tending to his injuries."

"Good. I'm on my way to the inn to pick you up, then we'll head over there."

"I'll be ready when you get here. Oh, and, Dillon?"

"Yes?"

"I'm sure this goes without saying, but aside from Chief Boyer, don't mention the attack to anyone around the station."

"Wait," he said. "Did I just hear you correctly? Did the queen of investigative journalism, who leaked top secret information regarding this case to the entire nation, just tell *me* to keep my mouth closed?"

"Don't start with me, Detective Reed!" Mona shot back. "Now hurry up and get here so we can go check on Oliver. We've got a case to solve."

"Yes, ma'am. I'll stop by Chief Boyer's office to give him a quick update, then I'll be on my way."

"Great. See you soon."

And with that, Dillon charged out the door.

DILLON AND MONA approached the Whitmans' front door and rang the bell.

As soon as it opened, he heard Oliver yell out in what sounded like excruciating pain.

"Mo-o-om!"

"I'll be there in a moment!" Mrs. Whitman called out over her shoulder before turning to Dillon and Mona. "Thank you so much for coming," she sniffled.

"Hello, Mrs. Whitman," he said quietly, relieved when she didn't react negatively to him being there.

Mrs. Whitman's watery eyes were a dark shade of pink. The tip of her runny nose was red. Her hands trembled as she wiped away the tears streaming down her cheeks.

"Please," she said, stepping to the side, "come in. Oliver is resting inside the study. Mr. Whitman is upstairs consulting with our attorney. But he should be down soon. Oh, and just to warn you, Oliver has converted the study into his own personal command center. So beware of all the clutter."

Dillon and Mona entered the house and followed Mrs. Whitman down a long hallway lined with dark, shiny hardwood floors and family portraits.

"Thank you for calling me," Mona told her. "I am so sorry that this happened to—"

"Mo-o-om!" Oliver called out once again.

Mrs. Whitman approached the study door.

"I appreciate that, Mona. We'd better go on in. I'll see what Oliver needs, and you two can talk to him about the assault." She paused, her voice quaking. "You have *got* to figure out who's behind these attacks on my family."

When she broke down in tears, Dillon gently placed his hand on her arm.

"We will," he told her. "We're getting closer and closer by the day."

He glanced over at Mona. Her eyes appeared glazed over, as if her mind were elsewhere. Dillon sensed she was thinking back on being attacked at the inn.

As Mrs. Whitman led them inside the study, he gave Mona's shoulder a reassuring squeeze.

"You okay?" he whispered.

She turned to him and nodded her head.

"Good."

He walked inside the dimly lit study. The oval-shaped room was lined with shelves filled with leather-bound books. A wrought iron chandelier hung from the high beam ceiling.

Piles of newspapers, file folders and computer print-outs were scattered everywhere. Three laptops had been set up on Victorian-style walnut end tables. Half-empty glasses and crumb-filled plates were strewn on the floor around a dark brown tufted leather couch.

And there, sprawled out across the sofa, was Oliver.

Dillon stopped dead in his tracks at the sight of him.

Both of Oliver's eyes were blackened and swollen. A stream of dried blood drained from his broken nose. His neck had been wrapped in a foam cervical collar. His right arm and left leg were heavily bandaged.

Dillon felt Mona grip his arm.

As shaken up as he was over Oliver's condition, he forced himself to remain calm and collected.

He cleared his throat, slowly approaching the couch.

"Hey, man," he said quietly. "How are you feeling?"

"Like crap," Oliver moaned. "Mom! Bring me a

glass of orange juice. With *no pulp* in it this time. And one of those painkillers Dr. Moore brought me."

"Sure, son," Mrs. Whitman breathed.

She walked over to the couch and collected a few of the dishes.

"Can you please hurry up?" Oliver yelled before wincing in agony. "I feel like I'm about to die!"

Mrs. Whitman covered her mouth. Dillon could tell she was struggling to hold back a sob.

"I'll be right back," she choked before rushing out of the room.

Mona took a deep breath and stepped forward.

"I'm so glad you called me over, Oliver. Thank you again. Detective Reed and I are determined to find out who did this to you. We both think the answer is going to get you justice, and also lead us to Olivia."

"Detective Reed," Oliver snorted. "What the hell is he doing here? I didn't invite him over. Just you. You're defying the fellow conspiracy theorist code, Mona. We're a secret society. You can't break the unspoken bond we're supposed to share."

"I know," Mona sighed dramatically, staring down at the floor as if she were disappointed in herself. "But considering the extenuating circumstances we're under, I didn't think you'd mind me breaking the code just this once. Time is running out, Oliver, and things are escalating. The perpetrator is getting more dangerous. We have got to get him off the streets before someone loses their life."

"If I worked for Lake Landry PD," Oliver said, "I would've had this case solved *weeks* ago."

Dillon bit his tongue, refusing to take the bait.

"Is it okay if we sit?" he asked, pointing over at the love seat positioned next to the couch.

"Whatever…"

Just when the pair sat down, Mrs. Whitman came scurrying into the room carrying a tray filled with orange juice, coffee and ice water.

"Mona, Dillon, I am so sorry," she said. "I didn't ask if you two wanted anything. I hope coffee and distilled water are enough for now. I need to get upstairs and speak with my husband and our attorney. But if you'd like anything else, just let me know."

"This is more than enough," Mona told her. "Thank you."

"You're welcome."

She handed Oliver his glass of orange juice and pain medication, then hurried out of the room.

As she closed the door behind her, Dillon pulled out his notepad.

"So did you get a look at your attacker?" he asked Oliver.

"Yeah. He was short and fat and dressed in all black tactical gear. Ballistic helmet and all. I should've been able to take him down. But he caught me off guard."

"How so?" Mona questioned while typing notes in her cell phone app.

"When I was getting inside my car, he rushed me from behind. I tried to pull out some of my Krav Maga moves on him, but he tackled me to the ground so fast that I didn't even get a chance."

"What is 'Krav Maga'?" Mona asked.

Dillon waited for Oliver to respond. But when he was hit with a coughing fit, Dillon turned to Mona.

"Krav Maga is an Israeli hand-to-hand combat system that was founded in 1891," Dillon said. "It was developed for defense and security forces."

"How do you even know that?" she asked.

"I actually learned about it not too long ago while watching an old episode of *Jeopardy*—"

"Dude!" Oliver interrupted. "First of all, the lady was talking to me. Secondly, why are you here again?"

Mona quickly reached over and placed her hand on Dillon's thigh before he could respond.

"Did you recognize anything else about your assailant?" she asked. "Despite the tactical gear, did his physique appear familiar? Or what about his voice? Did it sound familiar?"

"Mona, I'm not gonna lie to you. I smoked some weed before leaving the house. I wanted to be nice and mellow when I went down to the station to be interrogated. So no. I didn't recognize a thing. Not to mention I was busy getting beaten in the back of the head with the butt of a gun."

"Wait, he pistol-whipped you?" Dillon asked.

"Yes. But thanks to the almighty universe, I'm so mentally enlightened that my cerebral strength parlayed into my physical endurance. I took that beatdown like a *champ*, bro."

Dillon watched Oliver closely as he spoke. Despite his tough exterior, his teary eyes and quivering hands told a different story. He saw right through him. Oliver was terrified.

"What exactly did the attacker say to you?" Mona asked.

"Ahh!" Oliver moaned, turning over onto his side and rubbing his lower back. "He said all types of crap."

"Such as?"

"Stuff like, you'd better back off of this investigation. Your sister hates you, so why would you risk dying over her? Keep your mouth shut unless you wanna be killed. Then before he slammed my head into the concrete, he said this was my first and final warning."

Dillon and Mona discreetly glanced at one another. When she gave him a knowing nod of the head, he knew they were both thinking the same thing.

Oliver's assailant was probably the same man who'd attacked her.

"So you didn't get a look at the attacker?" Dillon asked.

"No."

"If you had to guess, who do you think was behind this attack?"

Oliver took a deep, labored breath.

"Let's be honest," he began. "A man like me is gonna have enemies. I'm pretty outspoken when it comes to my otherworldly beliefs and conspiracy theories. Some nonbelievers could be behind this attack, and using Olivia's disappearance as a cover-up."

"Do you really think that's the case?" Mona probed skeptically.

"No…" Oliver muttered before tossing the pills inside his mouth and taking a gulp of orange juice. "I don't. I just thought it was worth mentioning. I fully believe that Blake Carter sent one of his goons after me."

"And why do you think he'd do something like that?" Dillon asked while vigorously scribbling notes in his pad.

"Because he's still mad at me for going off on his boy."

"Leo Mendez?" Mona chimed in.

"Yeah. That clown. Also known as Blake's lap dog. But really, if I may just cut through the BS, Blake probably killed my sister because he wants to be free and single. Marrying her was a good look for them both. But then the whole *marriage* thing got real. He was expected to be committed and faithful, but obviously he couldn't. Yet he also wanted it both ways. Cheat, but start a family. Pressure my sister to have a baby while entertaining a harem of women. Doesn't make sense, does it?"

Dillon stopped writing midsentence. He was shocked to hear Oliver say something sensible for once.

"It definitely doesn't make sense," Mona agreed.

Oliver struggled to prop himself up on his elbows before crying out in pain.

Within seconds, Mrs. Whitman came charging into the room.

"Mona, Dillon," she said, "I think that's enough for today. Oliver needs to rest. Were you able to get what you needed?"

"Somewhat," Dillon replied. "I think we were just on the cusp of getting some good insight. But I understand. Oliver does need time to recover."

He pulled out his phone and checked his text messages.

"A couple of my colleagues are out front processing the crime scene now. Mona and I will go check in with them, then follow up with you later today. How does that sound?"

"That sounds good," Mrs. Whitman replied. "Thank you very much, Detective Reed and Mona. We appreciate you both."

"You're so welcome, Mrs. Whitman," Mona said

before approaching the couch. She stepped gingerly in between Oliver's piles of documents.

"Thank you again for calling us over," she told him.

"Thanks for coming to check on me," he croaked, closing his eyes tightly while grabbing the back of his head.

Dillon waited for Oliver to make a smart remark about not inviting him. When he didn't, Dillon knew he must've been in an immense amount of pain.

As Mrs. Whitman exited the study, Dillon noticed Mona bend down and pick a file folder up off the floor.

"Hey, what is this?" she asked Oliver.

He squinted, struggling to see what was in her hand.

"Some file I swiped off an exec's desk on my last day at Transformation Cosmetics. I never bothered to look through it."

"Would you mind if I take it with me? You never know. It may contain some pertinent information."

"Yeah, whatever," Oliver sighed before slumping down against the back of the couch.

"Thanks. Detective Reed and I will be in touch." Mona gave his shoulder a gentle pat, then walked toward the doorway.

"What was that all about?" Dillon asked her as they headed down the hallway.

"I spotted this folder labeled Transformation Cosmetics: Confidential *lying on the floor.* I have no clue what's in it, obviously. But I figured it was worth checking out."

"Good call. Once we get back to the inn, we'll do just that."

Chapter Sixteen

Mona sat next to Dillon on the teal blue silk love seat inside her room.

"There's nothing here," she mumbled, shuffling through the papers piled inside the Transformation Cosmetics file.

"Nothing?" Dillon asked. "Are you sure?"

"Well, nothing pertaining to Olivia's disappearance. All I see are promotional materials for community service events that the company hosted, a few inventory lists and a bunch of shipment receipts."

Dillon leaned over and scanned the papers.

"Interesting. Look at the bottom of each page. According to the URL, each of these documents is linked to Leo Mendez."

"Okay, but I don't see anything incriminating here."

Just as Mona continued paging through the documents, her cell phone rang. She reached down and grabbed it off the coffee table.

"Oh, this is Mrs. Whitman. I hope everything's okay with Oliver," she said before answering the call. "Hello?"

"Mona!" Mrs. Whitman screamed. "Is Detective Reed still with you?"

"Yes, he's right here. Why? What's going on?"

Mona quickly switched the call over to speakerphone so that Dillon could listen in.

"Mr. Whitman and I just received an anonymous phone call from a man claiming to have Olivia in his possession. He said that in order for our daughter to be returned to us safely, we must wire five million dollars into an offshore bank account by midnight tomorrow!"

Mona grabbed Dillon's arm. Tears of relief filled her eyes at the thought of Olivia still being alive.

But her heart pounded out of her chest as she wondered what her friend had been through since she'd gone missing.

"Mrs. Whitman," Dillon said, "did you make any sort of agreement with the kidnapper?"

"No. He didn't give us a chance to. He just passed along the banking information and said he'd call back in an hour with further instructions."

"Did he provide you with any proof that he really has Olivia in his possession?" he continued. "Did he let you speak to her?"

"No," Mrs. Whitman sobbed. "And I asked, but he wouldn't allow it. He said all I need to be concerned with is getting the money together. And if in an hour I have proof that I've begun the wire transfer process, he'll let me speak with Olivia."

"Well, by the time he calls back," Dillon told her as he began texting away on his cell, "I'll have a recorder set up on your phone. I'm sending Chief Boyer a message now letting him know what's going on. He'll obtain an emergency court order so we can put surveillance on the kidnapper's phone. We'll trace where the call is coming from, either through the VPN or cell phone towers. Mona and I will be there to help walk you through the conversation when he calls back."

"Thank you, Detective Reed. I'd definitely feel better having you two here with us. And I think you've got a good plan in place. Mr. Whitman, however, thinks otherwise. He'd like to speak with you."

Mona heard the phone rustling before Mr. Whitman got on the line.

"Detective Reed, I don't think it's a good idea to entertain this...this *criminal*. What if he's lying? What if this is all a scam, and the person doesn't really have our daughter? See, I knew the minute we went to the media with this case, fraudsters would come out of the woodwork, lying and demanding money."

"Mr. Whitman, that's a chance we're going to have to take," Dillon told him as Mona nodded her head in agreement. "This is the first lead we've gotten of this nature. And we need to act on it. Because what if it *is* legit, and this person does have your daughter? The only way we'll find out is by taking the necessary steps to try to get her back."

When Mr. Whitman responded with a disapproving grunt, Mona chimed in.

"Detective Reed is right, Mr. Whitman. I've worked on several missing person cases that involved ransom demands. You don't have to go through with the wire transfer. But you should at least begin the process to show that you're serious about sending him the money and bringing Olivia home."

"I don't know about all that," Mr. Whitman grumbled.

"Listen," Dillon said, standing up and grabbing his keys, "Mona and I are on our way there now. We'll have the house and your phone lines under surveillance. Trust me, we will get to the bottom of all this and, ultimately, get your daughter back."

"And what about the money wire transfer?" Mr. Whitman asked. "What should we do about that?"

"I'll have my digital forensic specialist pose as your banker and send you an email making it appear as though the transfer is in motion. That'll buy us some time while we work on locating the kidnapper."

"Fine," Mr. Whitman replied. "We'll see you when you get here."

Mona disconnected the call and grabbed her laptop.

"Hey," Dillon said. "Why don't you bring that Transformation Cosmetics folder you got from Oliver? We'll take a closer look at it and see what we can find."

"It's already in the bag."

"I should've known," he told her as they hurried out of the room and down to the lobby.

"I cannot believe this," Mona panted as the pair climbed inside the car. "We're finally going to solve this case, Dillon. I can feel it."

"I hope so…"

Mona sat at the Whitmans' dining room table. Every muscle in her body was wrought with tension.

She peered over at Mrs. Whitman, who was on the phone with the alleged kidnapper. Mr. Whitman sat next to her with his arm wrapped tightly around her shoulder.

"This email looks legit," the assailant said.

"Turn up the volume," Dillon whispered to Donovan, his digital forensic specialist.

Donovan nodded his head and increased the sound on the speakerphone.

"But I'm going to have to look into the transfer routing number," the assailant continued.

Mona shivered at the sound of his deep, distorted tone. It was obvious he was speaking through a voice enhancer. His garbled pitch was disturbing to say the least.

Mrs. Whitman crossed her arms in front of her tightly. She eyed Dillon wearily. He gave her a reassuring thumbs-up. She took a deep breath and leaned into the table.

"The email *is* legit," Mrs. Whitman said. "The routing number and all. Our banker is working to get the five million dollars wired to your account as we speak. Now, *please*. We're doing our part. You must do yours. Let us talk to our daughter!"

The kidnapper chuckled into the phone. "Tsk tsk, not so fast, Mrs. Whitman. According to this email, the transfer is still in the very early stages. You'll speak to your daughter once I see those funds moving."

"Just let me hear her voice," Mrs. Whitman sobbed. "*Please*. I'm begging you!"

Mona heard a click. The phone went dead.

"Let me speak to my daughter!" Mrs. Whitman screamed.

"He hung up," Dillon told her. "I'm so sorry."

Mrs. Whitman jumped up from the table.

"I can't do this," she wept. "I'm going to check on Oliver."

Mona's heart broke as she watched Mrs. Whitman rush out of the room. She turned to Donovan, who was busy typing away on his laptop.

"Were you able to pick up on a location?" she asked him.

"I'm communicating with the caller's cell phone service provider now. Her software application is tracking his phone's GPS positioning. She's keeping me updated as she goes. I'll let you know as soon as she gets a hit."

"Great. Thank you."

Mona wiped her damp forehead and turned to Dillon, whose head was buried in his cell phone.

"Just texting back and forth with Chief Boyer," he told her, as if sensing her anxiety. "He's down at the forensics lab waiting on the results of the DNA that was collected from the area where Oliver was attacked."

"Well, unlike the areas where I was attacked," Mona said, "I hope they're able to recover some sort of evidence."

"Let's hope so. In the meantime, why don't you take another look at the Transformation Cosmetics file? Between that and this trace we've put on the assailant, we're bound to get a hit."

"Good idea."

Mona pulled the file from her tote bag, glad for the distraction. Even though there didn't appear to be anything worthwhile in the folder, she hoped that paging through it would help ease her racing mind.

A loud clapping reverberated through the room. Mona jumped in her seat.

"We got a ping off a cell phone tower!" Donovan exclaimed.

Dillon pumped his fist in the air.

"Yes! What area are we looking at?"

"The phone is pinging about fifteen miles west of Lake Landry. Looks like it's moving toward the town rather than away from it. So our kidnapper is heading this way. The cell phone service provider is working to get an exact location."

"Excellent," Dillon told him. "As soon as she does, let me know."

"Will do."

Mona felt her heart thumping out of her chest. A rush of adrenaline flowed through her veins.

They were getting closer. Olivia would be home soon.

She hoped…

Dillon reached over and gave her hand a squeeze, snapping Mona out of her thoughts.

"Hey," he whispered, "I'm gonna step outside for a second and call Chief Boyer. He wants to discuss the likelihood of us recovering Olivia alive. I don't want to have that conversation in front of her family."

"Okay. While you do that, I'll continue combing through this file."

"Sounds good. Be right back."

After Dillon left the room, Mr. Whitman stood up.

"I'm going to go check on my wife and son," he muttered. "Maybe get a drink. Something strong, to help ease my mind. Would either of you like anything?"

"No, thank you," both Mona and Donovan replied in unison.

Her stomach churned at the sight of Mr. Whitman slinking out of the room. She and Donovan exchanged sympathetic looks. He turned back to his laptop, and she turned back to the file.

Mona once again thumbed through the random documents. Inspection reports and distribution plans were sandwiched between dispatch authorizations and fumigation statements.

"There is nothing here," she mumbled to herself.

Right before Mona slammed the file shut, she noticed a crumpled piece of paper stuck to the back of the folder.

Another receipt, she thought.

Mona pulled the document from the file, expecting to see a shipment confirmation.

But when she unfolded it, she laid eyes on a chain of email messages.

"I'm back," Dillon said, rushing into the room. He sat down next to Mona and flipped through his notepad. "Did I miss anything?"

"Nope," Donovan told him. "Mr. Whitman went to check on his family. I'm still waiting to hear back from the cell phone provider. And the creepy kidnapper hasn't called back yet."

"I may have found something," Mona said, sliding the email printout toward Dillon. "Take a look at this."

He leaned over, and together they scanned the document.

"You found this in Oliver's file?"

"Yes. It looks like several email exchanges between one of Transformation Cosmetics' general mailboxes and some random person who goes by the name GDub. The messages are short and cryptic. Like this one." She pointed. "'Materials picked up and discarded. Monies received.' There are several more that are worded the exact same way. The only difference is the dates they were sent to Transformation."

"Hmm, interesting…"

"Sorry to interrupt, guys," Donovan said, "but we've got movement."

Dillon hopped up from his chair and peered over Donovan's shoulder at the laptop.

"Talk to me. What are we looking at?"

"The kidnapper's phone is pinging on the border of Lake Landry. He's moving into town via St. Francis Boulevard."

Dillon grabbed his keys and cell phone.

"Donovan, Mona and I are going to track him down. Can you provide me with real-time updates while we head his way?"

"Absolutely, sir."

Mona felt a rush of energy jolt through her body. She shoved the email inside her tote bag.

"You ready?" Dillon asked her.

"I'm ready. Let's go."

Chapter Seventeen

Dillon turned up the volume on his car's Bluetooth.

"Talk to me, Donovan. Which way are we going?"

"Make a right turn down Armitage Street. But keep your distance. The kidnapper is slowing down toward the end of the block."

"You got it," Dillon replied.

He turned the corner and let up on the accelerator.

Mona leaned forward, squinting as she struggled to see through the darkness.

Streetlights were sparse on the upscale residential street. Sprawling lawns surrounded grand plantation-style homes.

The dark sedan that the kidnapper was driving decelerated up ahead.

Mona gripped the door handle. She resisted the urge to jump out of the car and rush his vehicle.

"I want to run up there and see if Olivia's inside of that car so badly," she told Dillon.

"Same here. But we have to be careful. If Olivia is in there, we don't wanna make a wrong move and jeopardize her safety."

"I know," Mona huffed. "We're just so close. My

anxiety is through the roof. I need to know that she's okay."

"Me, too. Hey, Donovan, has the kidnapper called the house again?"

"No, not yet."

"Okay. Looks like he's coming to a stop up ahead. Mona and I are sitting back toward the opposite end of the block with our headlights off."

"Good," Donovan replied. "Be sure to keep your distance."

"How are the Whitmans doing?" Mona asked.

"The best that they can. They're still in the study with Oliver. I told them to just stay in there and relax. I'll send for them if the kidnapper calls back."

"Good plan," Dillon told him. "Their stress levels appear to be at an all-time high, which is understandable. Just reassure them we're doing all that we can to bring Olivia home safely."

"I will."

Mona jumped when she felt her cell phone vibrate inside her pocket. She pulled it out and saw a text message notification appear on the screen from a number she didn't recognize.

"Who is this?" she muttered before opening and scanning it.

"Got some new intel?" Dillon asked.

"Wait. Let me read this message again."

Mona held her breath, rereading the message twice before almost dropping the phone.

"You are *not* gonna believe this," she said.

"Believe what?"

"I just got a text message from Emily at Alnico. Apparently, George Williamson has been conducting official Alnico business from his personal email address. And guess what name he goes by?"

"What nàme?" Dillon asked.

"GDub."

"GDub… Wait, isn't that the name of the person who was exchanging messages with someone from Transformation Cosmetics?"

"Yes, it is," Mona confirmed.

"That's strange. Why would an aluminum corporation be doing business with a cosmetics company?"

"Good question. I have no idea. But I definitely think it's something we should look—"

Mona was interrupted by the sound of screeching tires.

She looked up and saw the kidnapper's sedan peel away from the curb.

"Dillon!" she yelled. "He's on the move!"

"I'm on it," he said, hitting the accelerator and speeding after him.

"Do you have eyes on our suspect, Detective?" Donovan asked.

"I do. I'm following him now."

"Good. I'm tracking him on my end, as well. So just know that you've got backup in case you lose him."

"Thanks."

"Looks like he's getting on the expressway," Mona breathed, her voice filled with panic.

"Where the hell is he going now?" Dillon muttered.

"I don't know, but I'm dying to get a look at him and see if Olivia's in that car."

"We'll both get a look at him soon enough. He has to stop off somewhere eventually."

Dillon trailed the kidnapper onto the highway. He

expertly maneuvered his car while their suspect weaved in and out of traffic.

Mona gripped the dashboard. She and Dillon rode in silence, the chase too intense for conversation.

The abductor eventually exited the expressway and drove toward a swampy rural area.

"What in the world…?" Mona uttered. "Where is he going?"

Her racing heartbeat thumped sporadically. She stared out at the vast, desolate fields. Her eyes were met with an eerie darkness.

Mona did not have a good feeling.

"I have no idea where we are right now," Dillon said. "Didn't even know this area existed."

"Me either," Mona told him. "Be careful. You're getting kind of close to the suspect. There's hardly anyone else out here, so we could easily be noticed."

Dillon eased up on the accelerator and put some distance between his car and the kidnapper's.

"Are you still with him?" Donovan asked.

"I am. This guy just turned down some narrow, bumpy road. There are no streetlights or signs. And as difficult as it'll be to see, I'm gonna turn off my headlights and do my best to continue following the subject."

"Good idea," Donovan told him.

Dillon hit the brakes as the car's tires dipped down into huge holes in the road.

Mona braced herself, struggling to not bang her head against the window.

"Damn," she murmured. "Talk about a road less traveled. These bumps feel more like craters. It doesn't seem like anyone should be driving out here."

"I agree. And that's probably why our perp chose

this destination. Whatever crimes he's committed would be well hidden."

Mona dropped her head in her hand.

"Lord, please don't let this man lead us to Olivia's body…"

"Come on, now," Dillon told her. "Don't think like that. Believe that we're going to recover Olivia safely."

Mona looked up ahead and noticed red brake lights flashing. She reached over and grabbed Dillon's arm.

"He's stopping," she screeched. "He's stopping!"

"I see him," he told her calmly as he pulled over to the side of the road and cut the engine.

Mona slid to the edge of her seat and peered through the windshield.

"This looks like an abandoned sugarcane field," she said, eyeing the tall stalks leaning against the side of the car.

"It does. And I think I see some sort of shack up ahead."

Mona wrung her hands, once again anxious to hop out of the car and see if Olivia was inside the vehicle.

"I wish this man would hurry up and get out of his car so we can move in on him," she said, now rocking back and forth in her seat.

"He will. Just stay calm."

As soon as the words were out of Dillon's mouth, the man opened his car door.

"Okay," Mona whispered as if the suspect could hear her. "He's moving!"

Dillon reached over and opened the glove compartment. He pulled out a Glock 22 and a pair of handcuffs.

Mona inhaled sharply.

Uh-oh, she thought. *This just got real…*

"Donovan," Dillon said, "you still there?"

"Yes, I'm here, Detective."

"Listen, our subject is on the move. Mona and I are going to go after him. I need for you to give Chief Boyer an update on what's happening. Tell him to be on alert, but don't send backup to the scene just yet. It's too desolate out here. I don't want our perp to know we're on to him. He may panic and do something stupid."

"Like hurt Olivia," Mona added. "If he hasn't already."

"I'll call him now, sir," Donovan said. "Be careful, and keep me posted."

"Will do."

Dillon disconnected the call. He and Mona stared straight ahead, waiting to see what the assailant would do next.

Within seconds, he jumped out of the car and ran toward the shack.

Dillon turned to Mona.

"You ready?"

"I'm ready."

"Okay. Stay low, step quietly and follow my lead. Got it?"

"Got it," Mona responded, her voice filled with determination. "Now come on. Let's go get our girl."

"Let's do it."

The pair quickly opened their doors and slipped out. They ducked down, watching as the kidnapper tore up the shack's rickety wooden stairs.

Mona looked over at Dillon. He motioned for her to follow him.

They tiptoed along the edge of the sugarcane field.

As they got closer to the run-down gray cabin, Dillon pulled Mona back into the stalks' long green leaves.

The pair watched as the shadowy figure pushed through the door.

They heard a loud scream come from inside the house.

Mona gasped, covering her mouth to stop her own scream.

Dillon grabbed her hand and pulled her out onto the gravelly road.

"We're going in!" he declared.

Mona stayed close while they ran toward the shack. Dillon drew his gun as they hovered near the doorway.

The suspect had left the door wide-open. Dillon peeked around the corner inside the house. Mona stood next to him, discreetly peering over his shoulder.

It took a few moments for her eyes to adjust. Odd pieces of dilapidated furniture were scattered around a shabby, dimly lit living room.

Mona recoiled when the kidnapper appeared from behind a closed door. He was wearing a black ski mask and tactical gear. She immediately recognized his silhouette. It was her attacker.

Dillon motioned to Mona that they were going inside. She stood straight up and gripped his arm.

The perp walked farther into the living room. There, standing behind him, was Olivia.

Mona willed herself not to run in and rescue her.

The kidnapper grabbed Olivia by the throat, pulling her face inches away from his.

"Those wire transfer details your parents sent?" he yelled. "They're fraudulent! Do those idiots think I'm stupid enough to release you before I get my money?

How does it feel to know your family doesn't care enough about you to pay a ransom that wouldn't put a *dent* in their fortune?"

Olivia whimpered as tears streamed down her face. She clutched his hands, struggling to pull them away from her neck.

"Just hang tight," Dillon whispered to Mona. "I'm waiting on the right time to go in."

Mona nodded her head, her eyes glued to Olivia.

"Don't your parents know that if they keep playing games with me, I will *kill* you?"

Olivia's face twisted with terror. She screamed out.

He jerked her to the side in an attempt to silence her. That's when she noticed Mona and Dillon hovering in the doorway.

"Mona!" she yelled.

Dillon quickly pushed Mona behind him, then pivoted, pointing his gun at the suspect.

"Police! Get your hands up!"

The abductor froze. Olivia dropped to the floor and crawled over to a dingy floral couch in the corner of the room.

"I said get your hands up!" Dillon repeated.

The kidnapper slowly began to raise his hands in the air.

"That's it," Dillon said, carefully stepping inside the shack. Mona followed closely behind him.

"Do you have any weapons on you?" Dillon asked.

The perp remained silent.

"I said, do you have any weapons on you?"

Just when Dillon took a step toward him, the perp swiftly reached back inside his waistband.

Dillon cocked his gun.

The assailant pulled out a silver Beretta 92FS.

Just as he aimed it at the detective, Dillon blasted a shot. The bullet hit the wall right behind the assailant's arm.

Mona screamed and dropped to the floor.

The assailant shot back. The bullet careened past Dillon's ear, barely grazing his lobe as it flew out the door.

"Drop your weapon!" Dillon demanded.

The kidnapper fired another shot. As Dillon fired back, the perp spun around and bolted out the back door.

"Stay here!" Dillon told Mona and Olivia before charging after him.

Mona stayed low, crawling over toward the couch.

Olivia's eyes were wide with shock. She remained crouched down, frozen in fear.

"Olivia," Mona whimpered, embracing her friend tightly. "You have no idea how happy I am to see that you're alive! Are you okay?"

"I—I don't know…"

She leaned into Mona, her frail body shaking as she sobbed uncontrollably.

Mona glanced down at her friend. Olivia had lost a considerable amount of weight. Her dingy white T-shirt and baggy gray leggings hung off of her feeble frame.

Olivia's long, wavy hair was pulled back into a tangled ponytail. Her face was red and puffy, and her tired eyes were swollen. It was clear that she'd been through hell.

"Is that Detective Reed with you?" Olivia sniffled.

"Yes, it is. We've been working together for weeks trying to find you. He's been amazing."

"Well, then, let's go make sure he's okay," Olivia insisted, scrambling to stand up.

Mona had been so focused on Olivia that she'd forgotten Dillon was outside trying to capture the kidnapper.

A lump of terror formed in her throat at the thought of losing him.

She and Olivia ran out onto the shack's ragged back porch.

In the distance, Mona saw Dillon splashing through the dark, murky swampland. The gunman was several feet ahead of him.

"Be careful, Dillon!" Mona screamed at the sight of the chaotic chase.

She watched as he propelled his body forward and pounced on the kidnapper.

An intense brawl ensued. The pair thrashed about the muddy water. Fists flew in the air and vicious kicks were thrown.

Mona and Olivia clung to one another, looking on in horror.

The brutal attack seemed to go on forever. Mona covered her eyes, terrified of what would come next.

And then, a gunshot rang out.

Mona's eyes flew open. Both men collapsed into the water.

She gasped. Then froze. Waited to see if Dillon would stand up. When he didn't, Mona tore down the stairs.

"No, come back!" Olivia yelled, grabbing her arm. "You can't go out there. It's too dangerous!"

"But I have to check on Dillon," Mona cried.

"You can't," Olivia insisted, wrapping her arm

around her tightly. "Detective Reed is perfectly capable of taking care of himself. He'll be fine. Let's just wait here, where it's safe."

Mona stumbled back up the stairs. She willed herself not to unravel as she waited for Dillon to reemerge.

He's okay. Don't worry. He's okay...

She kept her eyes peeled to the marsh, holding her breath. Finally, the two men resurfaced.

"Oh thank God!" Mona cried out.

"He got him." Olivia wept as Dillon put the assailant in handcuffs and dragged him back through the thick wetland. "He got him..."

Mona broke down in tears and turned to Olivia. The two friends embraced one another once again.

"I cannot believe this is finally over," Mona sobbed. "And I can't wait to find out who this maniac is behind the mask."

Olivia's arms fell down by her sides. She pulled away from Mona, her expression perplexed.

"What do you mean, find out who he is?" she asked.

"What I mean is, we've been trying to catch that lunatic for weeks. He's attacked me on more than one occasion, and even tried to kill me after I refused to stop investigating your case. Then he beat your brother half to death. I want this coward's identity revealed so I can look him in the eye and show him that he didn't get the best of us."

"Mona," Olivia said quietly, "I thought you knew who'd captured me, and law enforcement was just trying to hunt him down."

"I have no idea who he is. He's been running around town hiding behind that creepy ski mask."

Mona watched as a veil of anger covered Olivia's

eyes. Her chin began to quiver as her chest heaved uncontrollably.

It was then that Mona realized she knew her captor.

"Olivia, who is he?" she whispered.

"Leo. Leo Mendez."

Chapter Eighteen

"Just so we're clear," Dillon said, watching as Mona poured the bottle of red wine into their glasses. "Leo Mendez of Transformation Cosmetics had established an underground agreement with George Williamson of Alnico Aluminum Corporation."

"That is correct," Mona replied, handing Dillon his glass.

"And we're *sure* that Blake Carter didn't know anything about this agreement."

She nodded her head.

"Right. He knew nothing about it. And that can be proven through email messages and records Blake kept."

Dillon took a long sip of wine, then sat down on the love seat inside of Mona's hotel room.

"You know, I was so busy interrogating Leo that I really didn't get a chance to speak with Olivia. But I'm glad you and Chief Boyer were there with her while she shared her story. So, tell me again. What was the purpose of this agreement?"

Mona sat down next to Dillon and leaned her head against his shoulder.

As he waited for her to answer the question, he subconsciously began stroking her hair.

Once he realized what he was doing, Dillon paused, waiting to see how she would react.

"Don't stop," Mona said softly. "That feels good."

"I won't," he replied as he continued running his fingers through her curls. "Now, what were you saying?"

"So, according to Olivia, Leo cut an under-the-table deal with Alnico to illegally dump Transformation Cosmetics' excess chemical waste. Blake had the paperwork to prove that he'd instructed Leo to hire a certified disposal service to safely discard the lead and chromium being produced during Transformation's manufacturing process. But Leo's secret agreement with Alnico was a much cheaper option that allowed him to drastically cut corporate costs. This enabled him to come in under budget, and the money he saved went directly toward his yearly bonus."

"Wow," Dillon breathed, staring up at the ceiling as he took it all in. "So Leo Mendez, Blake's right-hand man, the one he's always bragging about and propping up on a pedestal, sold him out and jeopardized the integrity of Transformation Cosmetics. All for a check."

"Exactly. But the arrangement between Leo and Alnico got out of hand when Leo instructed George to dump the chemicals into residential water sources. That's how Olivia discovered the acts of contamination. George wanted to meet with Olivia so he could blow the whistle on Leo. But Leo kidnapped her before she could find out the truth *or* report her findings to the government."

"And I'm guessing he planned to collect the ransom money and skip town before the truth came to light,"

Dillon added. "Luckily, we intercepted that plan before it came to fruition."

"Yes, we did, *partner*," Mona said, giving his thigh an affectionate squeeze.

Her touch caused him to shift in his seat. He took several sips of wine, then cleared his throat.

"I'm just glad we finally solved this case," he continued. "I got Leo to confess to Bonnie's murder, and Olivia has returned home safely. Oh, and judging by the way she and Blake were acting toward one another down at the station, they may even try to reconcile."

"Yeah, I noticed all that lovey-dovey action. I was shocked. But obviously they're both extremely traumatized by all of this. So if they can get past their issues and work things out, then good for them."

"I agree. And speaking of their trauma, I hope they'll be relieved knowing that Leo is in custody and George is being extradited back to the States from the Bahamas."

"I hope so, too," Mona said. "By the way, what are they being charged with?"

"They're both being charged with knowingly discharging hazardous substances into a water of the United States. In addition to that, Leo's been hit with kidnapping, attempted murder and extortion charges."

"Good."

Mona exhaled, then looked up at Dillon.

"You know I have to leave town soon."

"I do know that. And I'm trying not to think about it."

"Really? Why?"

"Because," Dillon said, gently brushing a strand of hair away from her eye, "it's gonna be tough not having you around. I've gotten used to you being here. And I really enjoy your company."

"That's nice to hear. I really enjoy your company, too."

The pair fell silent. After several moments, Mona sat up and turned to Dillon.

"Come home with me for Christmas."

"Wait, what?"

"You heard me. Come home with me for Christmas. Evergreen, Colorado, is amazing during the holidays. There's ice skating, caroling, holiday float parades, festivals…"

Dillon reached out and gently caressed her cheek.

"I would love to. But are you sure? Won't your entire family be there?"

"Yes, they will. And I'd love for you to meet them. You and I have been to hell and back together. We'll be the stars of Evergreen with all the stories we have to tell."

"I bet we would," he chuckled.

He and Mona gazed at one another.

"Thank you for the invitation," he said. "I'd be honored to spend Christmas with you and your family."

"The pleasure will be all mine," Mona murmured before they leaned into one another and shared a long, passionate kiss.

Epilogue

Three Months Later...

"A toast," Mona said, raising her glass of champagne in the air. "To Leo and George being convicted, this entire ordeal officially being over, and new beginnings."

"Salud."

Dillon clinked his glass against hers, then took a sip of champagne.

Mona sat back in her lounge chair and looked out at the setting sun.

She and Dillon were sitting out on her LA loft's rooftop deck, enjoying the scenic views of the vast, twinkling city.

He reached out and took her hand, interlocking his fingers with hers. She turned to him and smiled, still feeling as though it was all a dream.

"Can you believe that you're no longer a detective?" Mona asked him.

"You know, I can, actually. I don't think I realized how burned-out I was when I took the job with Lake Landry PD. By the time we'd solved Olivia's case, I was *done*. Working as a private investigator and setting my own schedule suits me much better."

"And so does LA living, doesn't it?"

"Yes, it does. But I have to admit, I would've gone anywhere in the world if it meant being with you."

"Aw, babe." Mona smiled, leaning over and planting a soft kiss on Dillon's lips. "I'm so glad you decided to move here. I never would've thought investigating my friend's disappearance would lead to me finding love, landing my own nightly news show—"

"And don't forget getting your man a job as a CNB News on-air contributor."

"That, too. Let's just say that I'm happy. And finally fulfilled."

Dillon wrapped his arm around Mona.

"I love hearing that," he said. "And I can say the same for myself. I never would've thought I'd leave Louisiana behind and find happiness elsewhere."

"But since you're consulting with police departments all over the state of Louisiana, you do still have roots there."

"I do. However, my heart is now deeply rooted here. With you."

Dillon leaned over and nuzzled her ear.

"I love you, Mona Avery."

She turned to him, blinking rapidly as tears of joy filled her eyes.

"I love you, too, Dillon Reed."

* * * * *

#2043 PURSUED BY THE SHERIFF
Mercy Ridge Lawmen • by Delores Fossen
The bullet that rips through Sheriff Jace Castillo's body stalls his investigation. But being nursed back to health by the shooter's sister is his biggest complication yet. Linnea Martell has always been—and still is—off-limits. And the danger only intensifies when Linnea gets caught in the line of fire...

#2044 DISAPPEARANCE AT DAKOTA RIDGE
Eagle Mountain: Search for Suspects • by Cindi Myers
When Lauren Baker's sister-in-law and niece go missing, she immediately has a suspect in mind and heads to Eagle Mountain, where she turns to Deputy Shane Ellis for help. And when another woman seen with her family is found dead, their desperate pursuit for answers becomes even more urgent.

#2045 COWBOY IN THE CROSSHAIRS
A North Star Novel Series • by Nicole Helm
After attempting to expose corruption throughout the military, former navy SEAL Nate Averly becomes an assassin's next target. When he flees to his brother's Montana ranch, North Star agent Elsie Rogers must protect him and uncover the threat before more lives are lost. But they're up against a cunning adversary who's deadlier than they ever imagined...

#2046 DISAVOWED IN WYOMING
Fugitive Heroes: Topaz Unit • by Juno Rushdan
Fleeing from a CIA kill squad, former operative Dean Delgado finds himself back in Wyoming and befriending veterinarian Kate Sawyer—the woman he was once forced to leave behind. But when an emergency call brings Kate under fire, protecting her is the only mission that matters to Dean—even if it puts his own life at risk.

#2047 LITTLE GIRL GONE
A Procedural Crime Story • by Amanda Stevens
Special agent Thea Lamb returns to her hometown to search for a child whose disappearance echoes a twenty-eight-year-old cold case—her twin sister's abduction. Working with her former partner, Jake Stillwell, Thea must overcome the pain that has tormented her for years. For both Thea and Jake, the job always came first...until now.

#2048 CHASING THE VIOLET KILLER
by R. Barri Flowers
After witnessing a serial killer murder her relative live on video chat, Secret Service agent Naomi Lincoln is determined to solve the case. But investigating forces her to work with detective Dylan Hester—the boyfriend she left brokenhearted years ago. Capturing the Violet Killer will be the greatest challenge of their lives—especially once he sets his sights on Naomi.

HICNM1221

"If need be, I could run my way out of these woods. You can't run," Linnea added.

"No, but I can return fire if we get into trouble," Jace argued. "And I stand a better chance of hitting a target than you do."

It was a good argument. Well, it would have been if he hadn't had the gunshot wound. It wasn't on his shooting arm, thank goodness, but he was weak, and any movement could cause that wound to open up.

"You could bleed out before I get you out of these woods," Linnea reminded him. "Besides, I'm not sure you can shoot, much less shoot straight. You can't even stand up without help."

As if to prove her wrong, he picked up his gun from the nightstand and straightened his posture, pulling back his shoulders.

And what little color he had drained from his face.

Cursing him and their situation, she dragged a chair closer to the window and had him sit down.

"The main road isn't that far, only about a mile," she continued. Linnea tried to tamp down her argumentative tone. "I can get there on the ATV and call for help. Your deputies and the EMTs can figure out the best way to get you to a hospital."

That was the part of her plan that worked. What she didn't feel comfortable about was leaving Jace alone while she got to the main road. Definitely not ideal, but they didn't have any other workable solutions.

Of course, this option wouldn't work until the lightning stopped. She could get through the wind and rain, but if she got struck by lightning or a tree falling from a strike, it could be fatal. First to her, and then to Jace, since he'd be stuck here in the cabin.

He looked up at her, his color a little better now, and his eyes were hard and intense. "I can't let you take a risk like that. Gideon could ambush you."

"That's true," she admitted. "But the alternative is for us to wait here. Maybe for days until you're strong enough to ride out with me. That might not be wise since I suspect you need antibiotics for your wound before an infection starts brewing."

His jaw tightened, and even though he'd had plenty trouble standing, Jace got up. This time he didn't stagger, but she did notice the white-knuckle grip he had on his gun. "We'll see how I feel once the storm has passed."

In other words, he would insist on going with her. Linnea sighed. Obviously, Jace had a mile-wide stubborn streak and was planning on dismissing her *one workable option*.

"If you're hungry, there's some canned soup in the cabinet," she said, shifting the subject.

Jace didn't respond to that. However, he did step in front of her as if to shield her. And he lifted his gun.

"Get down," Jace ordered. "Someone's out there."

Don't miss
Pursued by the Sheriff
by Delores Fossen, available January 2022 wherever Harlequin Intrigue books and ebooks are sold.

Harlequin.com

Get 4 FREE REWARDS!

We'll send you 2 FREE Books plus 2 FREE Mystery Gifts.

Harlequin Intrigue books are action-packed stories that will keep you on the edge of your seat. Solve the crime and deliver justice at all costs.

FREE Value Over **$20**

IF YOU ENJOYED THIS BOOK
WE THINK YOU WILL ALSO LOVE

HARLEQUIN
ROMANTIC SUSPENSE

Danger. Passion. Drama.

These heart-racing page-turners will keep you guessing to the very end. Experience the thrill of unexpected plot twists and irresistible chemistry.

4 NEW BOOKS AVAILABLE EVERY MONTH!

"All of that's true and I hate this has happened to you," Maxwell said. "But you've forgotten one important fact. You weren't harmed. At least not physically. Everything in that house can be replaced."

"That might be true, but—"

"But you—" he kissed the side of her forehead "— sweetheart, you're irreplaceable, and I'm glad you weren't hurt. Now, *that*? That would've made the evening a helluva lot worse. Because if that had happened, I would be out for blood. We wouldn't be sitting here together because I'd be out hunting that bastard. Instead, we have others looking into the situation while you and I are getting ready to try to salvage our date. So how about we start by enjoying an excellent meal?"

After a long beat of silence, Amina sighed dramatically and leaned back to look up at him. A slow smile tugged the corners of her lips. "Well, when you put it that way, I guess I should pick a restaurant, huh?"

He grinned and handed her the menus. "Yes, and I'll take the bags upstairs, then change clothes. When I come back down, we can order." He stood and headed for the stairs again but stopped when she called him. "Yeah?"

"Thanks for coming to the house. It meant a lot to have you there with me even though I know it was the last place you wanted to be."

He studied her for a moment. "That might've been the case at first, but I want to be wherever you are, Amina. And I'll always be here, there or wherever for you. Remember that."

Don't miss
His to Defend *by Sharon C. Cooper,*
available January 2022 wherever
Harlequin Romantic Suspense
books and ebooks are sold.

Harlequin.com